EXIRE
HELEN
MORT

—

Exire

Helen Mort

ISBN 9781903110591

First published in this edition 2018 by Wrecking Ball Press.

Copyright Helen Mort

Cover design by humandesign.co.uk

Printed and bound in Great Britain by Clays Ltd, Elcograf S.p.A.

There is an evening coming in
Across the fields, one never seen before,
That lights no lamps.

- Philip Larkin, 'Going'

exire.com - our values:

Exire offers a range of options in an accessible format.
Exire offers a bespoke service that is discrete and professional.
Exire employs only the best writers.
Exire gives back the power to choose.
Exire looks after the needs of your family.

LORNA

I don't want to seem like I'm waiting. Nobody does. I get my phone
out of my pocket and pretend to look at it, but I just catch my
reflection in the dark screen. Too much eyeliner. The left eye slightly
smudged. My cheeks are hollow and my hair lies flat against my
head. As I slip it back into the pocket of my jacket, I hold the button
down. He won't call. He knows what I look like. I brush down the
sides of my jacket.

This is a place where people meet up, pair off and walk out
into the night, down Woodhouse Lane and into the chain
bars along the Headrow. The sun's sinking behind the brand
new library, lighting it orange. I watch two girls in furry
oversized jackets air-kissing. They link arms as they leave.
At the foot of the steps, there's a man in a tweed flat cap, the ironic kind.
A younger woman is walking towards him, spots him and quickens.
He does that thing where he pretends he hasn't seen her, looks at
his feet, glances up at the last minute. They kiss - a light, lingering
kiss - and he pulls her back towards the wall, drawing her in. Ginny
used to say you can tell when people are having an affair by the way
they kiss each other. She told me that in a railway station, watching
a couple in matching pinstripes grope, until the train blocked them
from view. When it pulled out from the platform, they were gone. *I
should know*, she said.

I am numb. My hands are like china. There's a girl on her own in a
parka, oversized glasses. She's smoking and as she exhales she looks
over at me. I must be staring. I put my head down but I can tell she's
still watching. Without moving, I know when she's stubbed the roll
up out with her trainer, when she's turned to walk into the library,
giving a last glance back. I keep my eyes fixed on the step in front.
I'm good at that. When I left the house this morning, I made myself

go without saying goodbye. Shut the door gingerly.

I know this is him approaching. I'm sure before he's reached the foot of the steps. I start to descend, very slowly.

"Lorna."

My name sounds strange in his mouth. Too sweet.

I'm not sure if I should shake his hand. "Nice to meet you."

His face is warmer than his photograph. A sculpted beard. Shock of dark hair.

"Drink? Do you know somewhere?"

I nod. I'm wearing a fake leather pencil skirt and it makes my steps tight, all the way into town. We don't speak until we get to Great George Street. The rain's coming down in smooth sheets now and he asks if I want an umbrella. I shake my head, step out into the road, and then a horn blares, a blur of water and I feel him drag me back onto the pavement. His grip on my waist is firm. I startle. I don't understand why he did that and for a moment, he looks as if he doesn't either. We carry on when it is safe.

In the bar, there's an A3 ale menu - all the beer names have puns and complicated descriptions. *A rich, malty stout. A citrusy pale.* There are a lot of women in here who dress the way I always thought I'd like to. He's asked me to order for him, and I lean over the counter top, trying to stand like them, watching him across the room. He sits as if he's happy. Not aware of how anyone might see him, his legs slightly apart, still wearing his denim jacket. If I met him in a club, I think I'd want him.

The barman has been asking *what can I get you, love?* and I've said nothing. I order two pints of Cascade and carry them back, trying to keep my hands steady.

He has a way of looking at me that makes me feel as if I'm sitting in a window, framed by grey light. All of his questions are polite, rehearsed. We talk about Ginny, talk about my childhood. I even mention my dad. He doesn't give anything away. I realise our knees are touching under the table and it feels better than anything has for months.

He leans across the table when he speaks, imperceptibly.

"Don't you want to know anything about me?"

I shred a beer mat into scraps. "No."

"I get that." He nods as if he really does. Then he says "I like it here."

"Not my scene, usually. I don't really go to the pub."

That isn't true. When I first met Sam, we were out every weekend. We'd catch the train to Saltaire and sit in the haphazard bar at Fanny's until kicking out time, sometimes not even talking, just being close, knowing we were sharing a corner.

"You must have played some places like this though, right?"

I smile with my lips together. I shouldn't have mentioned the band.

"We did our farewell gig down the road from here."

"What did you play? What was your last song?"

I shrug. "Does it matter?"

"I don't know."

I am silent for a long time. I'm back in the spare room with my tipped over waste paper basket and my frustrated hands on the table and the sad hum of the computer screen. I'm home alone and I'm speechless and I can't listen to the radio any more because it sends me mad. Even the idea of it, the music it holds, the way the songs have become a different language.

"It was called *Stockport Allegory*. It was shit."

"Sounds like one of these," he gestures to the menu. "A lively beer with a clean aftertaste."

I catch myself almost smiling.

"Something like that."

A drunk goth lurches over to our table and asks him if he has a light, so he pretends to pat his pockets. She puts the cigarette behind her ear, glances over at me, takes me in. Then she straightens herself up as if she's sober and gives me a wink.

"You make a good couple," she says, wiping her hands down on her black corset. "You look good." Then she laughs like a drain.

I don't feel like talking any more. His pint is three quarters empty and I've hardly touched mine. I wonder if he's supposed to drink.

"What time is it?" I ask. "Do you think we should go?"

He finishes his glass. "That's completely up to you, Lorna."

He puts his hand on my knee and squeezes. I tense, but I stare him out. Dark blue eyes. Hypnotic, not quite trustworthy. People with blue eyes always look as if they're flirting with you, even when they aren't. The last bassist was like that. He never shaved properly and when he looked at me, it hit me in the chest. When I was writing well, I used to write songs about things like that. Feelings, I mean.

There's a gaggle of men at the bar, they seem like they're from out of town. Brash but shifty. One of them keeps slapping the others on the back, slamming his glass down on the bar too hard. Towards the end, I was afraid of those men at gigs. People who stood at the back, carrying on their conversations, or near the front with their arms folded saying impress me. I always wished I was taller, more striking, or thinner and more mysterious, something that would give me a hold over them so they'd care less about my voice. I hated myself more than usual for feeling that way. I was terrified of men not noticing me but I was more scared they might.

"Let's go." He seems to see through me. He bites his lip. I realise with a lurch that he's nervous.

"Is it far?"

"Down Burley Road. We can take a cab if you want."

I don't. I want to walk out past those men with my head held high and my shoulders back, as if my thoughts are a drink too close to the edge of the glass. I want to share a silence with him all the way past the town hall and the hospital and the short-term lets and the scattered blue bins. I want it to be different from all the other silences I've kept.

We walk slowly as we get further from town. Under an old railway bridge, the moon shines brighter than the streetlamps. I am very aware of his neck. His height. The way he holds his arms as he walks. When the pavement narrows, he lets me go in front of him. I've been trying not to think about Sam but now I do. I remember the corners of his mouth, the smell of his oldest scarf, the shelf we built together where he hoarded all the books I ever sent him. I think of him on the wrong side of the bed, dozing, winding the duvet round his legs, not quite snoring but breathing in shudders. I imagine him waking and reaching out for me.

We're side by side again now, leaning into a hill, and his face is half-lit. It hasn't stopped being a strange face yet. I wonder if he has a girlfriend and what she thinks he's doing right now. I picture someone kind and not quite humourless, beautiful in an unassuming, softly-entitled sort of way. A small, snub nose. Delicate ears. Hair swept back and pinned up. I started to find my own face boring months ago. I stopped even disliking it.

The hired apartment is past a garage, the smooth glass and silver door numbers shine conspicuously amongst the red brick terraces and rundown corner shops and the scramble of trees. He is anxious now, fumbling for the key fob. I put my hand on the small of his back and I don't know why. We almost trip through the doorway. There's a neat, empty hallway that smells like a new car. He turns right and opens another lock.

The white corridor inside frightens me, but I don't say so. There are four shut doors and I want to try them all. Two bedrooms. A black and purple bathroom. A living room with a tidy kitchen at the end of it - an empty fridge with the door left open. On the worktop, a kettle and two mugs. The room focused around a black leather sofa. First, he draws the blinds and then he takes his jacket off and folds it on the arm.

"Do you want a cup of tea?" I realise I'm fumbling with the kettle cord.

He shakes his head. I blush. "I don't know why I asked you that."

I go over to the window and stand next to him and twitch the blinds, even though there's nothing to see except the road we've just come from. Midnight, shut inside the parked cars. I try to take his hand and he doesn't pull away.

"Are you sure you want to go through with this?" He doesn't turn to face me.

"What do you think?"

I let the blind go, let my other hand fall from his. He has never done this before. I don't know why I didn't realise sooner. On the website, his photo gave nothing away. Not even his name. But there was something about his face. Not quite smiling. Untidy hair.

I don't know how long we stand there for. My thoughts are a locked room. I'm completely calm now. I know he is shaking but I can't think about that.

When I've decided it's time, I go through into the bedroom and he follows me. I've selected this room, this way. There was a box on the website and I ticked it. There's nothing else to ask.

"Lorna - I just wanted to let you know how much I enjoyed tonight. I mean, how much I enjoyed talking to you."

I place a finger over his lips and he almost flinches.

"You don't need to say that."

I lie down on the bed, fully clothed. I tell him I am ready. I hear him move but the sound seems far away. His shadow falls sideways. Then

I feel the soft weight against me. The smoothness of the pillowcase.

He holds it down over my face. There is a kind of darkness. I hoped it would be like drifting into sleep, but it is not.

DON

I first met Gerry at a urinal. I'd hit rock bottom that week. It was an underground bar in Manchester, a place that used to be a public toilet and I remember thinking that made the piss I was having a postmodern piss. A piss within a piss. I didn't say that to Gerry. He was the one who always cracked the jokes.

*

These are some of the questions we ask: *what do you feel most indebted to your loved ones for? What is your greatest regret? Are there any people apart from your immediate family who you are especially close to? Is there a place that has particular significance in your life? Is there anything you'd like to apologise for? Which achievements are you most proud of?*

*

After our third pint, I told Gerry that I had a rough childhood. That's a lie. My parents are still together and we come from a street on the edge of an estate with a bad reputation. I'd skirt round those roads on the way back from school. When I told my folks I wanted to be a writer, they helped pay my tuition fees. Creative Writing. Nottingham. Nobody bullied me at school except myself.

My first and only play was called *God's Toothbrush*. It got a script-in-hand read-through in Salford and a scratch night performance at The Crucible. The problem was, the lead wasn't very convincing. He was supposed to be a psychopath but he was more like a cartoon villain. Nowhere near deadpan enough. If I wrote it again now, I'd probably base him on Gerry.

One of the things other writers never tell you is that, unless you're Hemingway, it helps if you're really fucking good looking and you can be in those Saturday spreads, saying things like *I only feel articulate when I'm speaking to The Muse*, or *everything I do is political*, standing on the edge of a moor you don't know the name of. And if you're not good looking, you'd better be a prize arse-licker, someone they'd call a Nice Guy. Writers never tell you this because they don't want to think about which category they fall into. Whether people buy their novels because they want to fuck them after the wine reception or because they think they can rely on them for a nice endorsement for their pamphlet with Gilded By Monkeys Press. I told my ex this and she said I should really talk to someone about my crippling cynicism. But that's because she had the kind of beauty people call 'haunted' and everyone wanted to sleep with her and eventually her agent did.

*

Verbal undertaker. That was the phrase he used. We'd had a line of coke each by then and we were acting like Gerry's flat was Wembley, saying everything to an invisible audience. I wouldn't normally have brought up money - it's easy to avoid the subject when you don't have any - but the coke was working my mouth like a puppet. If I'm honest, I just wanted to know how he funded his habit.

He showed me the website on his old school laptop. It was very discreet, took me a while to twig. It was a nice font, very clean-looking. He showed me some example letters, some of the quotes from relatives and friends. He was like a prefect taking someone round a school.

I noticed that his flat had nothing on the walls. Nothing at all. Most people have a calendar at least. There wasn't even a clock. It would have been an alright room if you made some effort with it.

High ceilings, Victorian. Gerry told me about his pen name, showed me his writer profile on the site. After that, he suggested we hired a prostitute.

*

I'm proud of some of them. I did this piece a few months back for a 47 year old man from Carlisle. Ex-farmer, lived with his mum after the divorce. In his notes, he mentioned hiking so I threw in a reference to one of the Lakeland fells. After that, I started Googling them, looking them up to make sure I'd got the names and spellings right. I've never been to Cumbria. There were all these images of the mountains, some of them half-covered in snow, like they'd been dipped in it. There was one called Skiddaw and the colours in the photo were almost unbearable - burnt orange and brown and pale gold. I found a line from Wordsworth, from *The Prelude* and I chucked that in as well. When I read it back, I thought it was the best thing I'd ever written. I've got it as my desktop background now. A mountain shaped like an arrowhead.

*

Please answer the questions as fully as you are able. The details you give will help us to make your letter personal and authentic. You may provide us with some examples of your own writing if you wish to help our experts emulate your style. These could include: letters, emails or even texts. We work with a dedicated and experienced team of creative professionals and we guarantee your family a service that is compassionate but forthright, something that will help them better understand your decision.

*

I had a girl back to mine last night. I know it's hard to believe. She came and sat opposite me on the last tram from Sale, even though the rest of the carriage was empty. She had dyed hair - satsuma orange - and these square, turquoise earrings. When we got home, we gave up on speaking and I was going down on her when she stopped me and held my face in both her hands and made me look at her and she asked me what I did for a living. Just like that. Like it was suddenly important that she knew. And for once, I just thought *fuck it*.

She didn't get it at first. She thought I meant I helped people commit professional suicide, screw up their jobs. Then she did and she pulled her jumper back over her head and took her coat from the back of the door where I'd hung it up really carefully and left. You should never be honest with anyone.

*

They say some people are born to do their job, teachers and doctors usually. I think Gerry was born for this. One minute he's got his palm flat on the table, talking to you like you're the only person in the room, the only person that matters. The next, he's locked himself in the bathroom and you have to let yourself out, or he'll just pick up a book while you're there and start reading. Oscar Wilde. That's his favourite.

Once, he broke an antique lamp over my head. It was very thin glass and it scattered like confetti. I'd been talking for too long and he wanted to interrupt me. He missed my face and it broke against the wall. It belonged to the last tenant so I wasn't too bothered. He's very good at what he does. A natural.

Me? I wasn't born to do anything.

JULIA

There's a part of Vancouver just outside Kitsilano - the hippy district I grew up in - where you drive towards the Burrard Street Bridge and the rest of the city is across the water, running parallel. Wherever you go, you feel as if it's keeping an eye on you. Or keeping up with you. At night, the lights make it what people call romantic. I suppose the name for it would be a spit of land, a long, slender stretch. But I've never liked that word very much.

I was trying to tell him about Kits and about how, when you look back on your life, it's a little like that. You think you're a new person, but really, the one you used to be is somewhere on the other side of the water and you can see it all the time. And you know there's a bridge connecting you if you want to take it. But he wasn't listening because he asked me:

"Is Vancouver really good for seafood? I heard that somewhere."

"Sure," I said "There are some nice places, downtown. If you've got the money."

He nodded, like he was making a note of it.

This was supposed to be the last time we were ever going to be together. I thought that would give it a kind of passionate urgency, but I just wanted to wrap myself in the hotel dressing gown and eat peanuts from the mini bar. His wife called twice and he ducked into the bathroom.

"You should be careful with that," I said after he came back the first time. "The echo."

He nodded. "Shit," he said. "You're right." He ran a hand through his hair with this wide-eyed expression and I remembered that when we were first introduced I thought he was a bit like Hugh Grant.

The second time, I asked "Is everything okay?" and he gave a tight smile.

"We're halfway through having the roof totally redone and the thatcher didn't turn up today. Thatch is an absolute nightmare. If I could go back, I'd buy a new build."

That's one of his favourite phrases. *If I could go back.* If he could rewind things, if he could have met me at a different time, if he could make life simpler. We both know that if he really could start over, he'd do exactly the same things.

He tries to slide his hand under the white robe, but I shrug him off.

"Do you think there's anything on TV?"

I pick up the remote and the screen fills with colour. Cartoon people the size of houses. At this time in the afternoon, it's all kiddy programmes.

"Are you hungry?" he asks.

"No. But I could eat."

I find it easier to be honest with him because he lies to me. My sister would say that I'm emotionally detached. I only like opinions from people who have no reason to judge me. Hairdressers. Call centre workers. I once bought a whole set of cashmere blend jumpers in dark grey from a store because a girl in a garage told me it was my colour. I got them that very same day. People who don't know you can tell what you need to hear. They see you. That's why my dentist knows more about me than my sister does.

Sometimes I say, *I work in a male-dominated industry. I'm what you might call a pioneer.*

He is busy at the hotel mini bar, stooped over, making himself a gin with ice.

"You want one?"

I shake my head.

I didn't need to tell him about my work because of the way we met. We never needed to have that conversation.

He stands up and stretches. Then he stops as if he's thought of something that bothers him and he goes back to the mini bar, opens the door and unscrews the jar of olives, plants a single one in his glass.

"Cheers," he says to the TV screen. "Good health."

The thing I like best about him is his voice. He sounds the way I always imagined someone from England would. I would like him to talk to me in darkness, forever. I go sit with him on the bed and I drape my legs across his lap. He strokes my calf and my shin, absently, runs his hand down over my feet, touches each of my toes in turn. He has large hands, capable.

"You know what they call gin?" he asks.

"Mother's ruin."

"Exactly."

"Good job we aren't mothers."

He puts the glass down on the glass cabinet, then lifts me so I've got my legs wrapped around his waist.

"Would you ever have kids, do you think?"

He's forgetting we've done this before. We have done all of this before in lifts and badly-lit wine bars and in coffee shops the next day.

I smile. "Would they ever have me?"

"You'd be a good mum."

"In a different life. Different job."

The night we met, that was one of the first things he told me about himself. Some of them aren't talkers, they want the whole thing to happen in silence, but he couldn't stop. We were in a room like this one, a hotel with piped opera music in the lobby and I got his life story in the first ten minutes. Two children. Four and seven. As the night unwound, that's what he kept coming back to. *I don't know if they'd ever forgive me.*

I've seen a photograph of them on his iPhone and I tried not to look too hard. The youngest one - Becky - is in denim dungarees and she's holding her hands up to the camera because she's got dough on them. Her mouth is open in a kind of grin. Rowan is in the background, shy, looking upwards. You can see that he has brown eyes.

I always notice their phones. Some people have a screensaver picture that I guess is the landscape that means most to them. A beach where they had their honeymoon. The sky through a thin wood.

A lake somewhere in Italy. Others have their wives and children. Husbands. Cats and dogs. All staring out from the screen as if they must have known something all along. The ones who have nothing frighten me most. Blue screens. Generic pictures of flowers. I bag the phones in plastic along with everything else. That's procedure.

He has finished his gin and he's fixing another. I take the dressing gown off and get into bed with the covers pulled high up to my neck. He stands in front of me and takes off the black t-shirt he was wearing and pulls down his boxers. Then he gets in beside me and we lie next to each other without touching.

"The thing I need you to know," he says. "Is that you saved my life."

I laugh. "No. You did that."

Soon he is on top of me, trying to make me look at him properly.

"I mean it, Jules."

When he fucks me, it's like he's trying to prove something. Afterwards, he presses himself against me and holds me a little too tight. He speaks into my neck, into my hair.

"Don't you ever think about doing something else?"

"What do you mean?"

"You know what. Another career. It's not a job..." He tails off.

"Not a job for a woman?"

When I signed up for this, that was part of the appeal. I'd scrolled through the website profiles a few times, looked at the photographs, the stern, dignified expressions. All men. At the interview, they practically begged me to accept. All of the panel except Mason. When they sent me outside so they could confer, I could hear him muttering through the thin plywood door. *Do you think she'll cope?* His voice was the loudest.

I thought of him the first time I shot a man in the head. Mason, I mean. Bursting out of his CEO's suit, strumming his fat fingers on the arms of his black swivel chair. I thought of him and I heard him asking me if I was married, if I planned to start a family in the next few years. I levelled and pulled the trigger.

The ones who choose pills are the hardest. I have to stay with them until I'm certain they're gone, make sure everything is in order. Sometimes I just sit next to them. Sometimes I hold their hand, depending on what they've ordered. Once, I tried to watch TV. It made me think about when I was a kid and mom would argue with my step-dad downstairs and I'd switch a programme on in my room and try to concentrate on it.

He's kissing the back of my neck now, lifting up my hair.

"I'm sorry," he says. "It really is none of my business."

I won't say how he wanted to go. But I'd prepared everything, of course. When he started to cry, I hesitated. I left it at least a minute before I put my hand on his shoulder. I'd never had a client cry on me before, which is uncanny when you think about it. When he kissed me, I thought I was going to cry too.

His phone rings again and he goes into the bathroom to answer it. I hear him saying *darling* and laughing. He is explaining he'll be back soon and he's telling the truth.

I go to the window and watch the street below. We are on the fifth floor, so it's a long way down. There is nothing much happening and I find that comforting. A woman with short trousers walking a fluffy white dog. A small poodle maybe. A bus waiting with its doors open, then pulling away. A man who seems like he's laughing.

My favourite bridge in Vancouver is the one you can't see from Kits. It's called Lion's Gate Bridge and it runs out to the North Shore, out to the park and the trees and everything beyond. If you crossed it and kept going, you might end up in Whistler - tall mountains with ski slopes. I never really went, but I used to like knowing it was there, evenings especially. The woods and the silence. Someone riding home into the city, or walking out into the night on the other side of it, not really knowing where they were off to. Someone talking to themselves. Someone saying *I swear* and *if I could go back.*

LORNA

Our very last rehearsal began with the bassist punching the drummer efficiently in the face. Dave strode into the room - a rented studio above an old foundry, peeling walls that are meant to be chic - put his bass down, walked calmly over to where Simon was leaning against the wall, texting, and spoke his name.

We all looked up, and Simon put his phone away.

"You're a Welsh cunt," said Dave. Then he clocked him, hard. It wasn't a particularly well-aimed punch, grazing Simon's chin. But it was quick and forceful. That morning was brilliant and it cast us all bronze, making the drum kit and the mic stand glint. Dave went over to the corner, unzipped the guitar case and started practicing the bassline for our new track. Within a few minutes, we'd all joined in with him. I enunciated every word, standing too close to the mic. Simon didn't get his phone out again for the rest of the rehearsal. His chin bloomed pink and he smiled. He was ugly. But he played the drums like a cat in a tumble dryer, putting his whole body into it, his whole frame.

I'm thinking of that punch now as I watch Dave balancing our coffees on a silver tray. Black Americano for me, over-sweetened latte for him. As if Dave's become a man who might be capable of moments of random violence, unpredictable tenderness. He is wearing a slogan t-shirt that says PARIS backwards. A woollen hat, pulled down close to his eyes.

He places the coffees on the table, slopping some over the sides, then he slams down a copy of a magazine next to it, open at a centre page. There is a photograph of a woman I hardly recognise, wearing her hair like mine, in my favourite mauve dress, mid-song.

"The Truth Scoop think we're shit," he says, jabbing a finger at the column. "Beg your pardon - they think we're 'melodically challenged.'"

My hands are shaking as I lift the mug to my lips and drink. I am down to one apple a day now and the warmth in my stomach is a shock, almost acidic. Yesterday, I fainted on the bus and blamed it on the heat. I pull my jumper down further over my wrists, stretching the sleeves.

"Melody Reckless? Seriously? What kind of a name is that?"

"It's a pseudonym for Si Delacruz. Used to write for the NME." He pauses, glances down at the coffee he's just remembered. "Once. He wrote for them once."

In the photograph, I'm not looking at the camera but my mouth is partly open, as if I'm waiting to be fed. *Open wide.* My dress clings to my hips, the obscene curve of my thigh, the bump of my arse. You can't see the audience, but I'm looking somewhere above them.

"What 'The More Deceived' fail to realise is that instrumentals the length of Christmas are only effective if your lead guitarist can play more than three chords. Lorna Malley excels as the pouty, troubled front woman, moody to the point of cliché," He's doing his 1950s newsreader voice. "An encore performance of their first single *Heartsore* is delivered with passable sincerity and excessive bass."

"Ouch." I am savouring my coffee, wondering if the heat of it will give me the energy to walk home. From the corner of my eye, I watch a couple at the next table dividing up a toffee muffin. The centre oozes out and pools into the case. She takes a bite and some of it dribbles down her chin. I think about picking up the paper and smelling it, just breathing it in. I remind myself I am not hungry. I have not been hungry for days.

"Excessive bass? What the fuck does that mean?"

"It means you made the fatal mistake of enjoying yourself."

"Piss off." He looms across the table. His breath smells savoury. "At least he liked you."

"Did he?"

"Everyone loves a moody front woman," His lip curls slightly, then he smiles slyly. "Especially if they think they're available."

The couple are feeding each other pieces of muffin, giggling. I can't stand people playing with their food. Girls who eat the outside of a chocolate bar before they eat the centre. Though that's exactly what I used to do when I still ate chocolate, making it last.

"We need some new material," I say, turning a teaspoon round and round in my hands. "Fresh songs."

"Too fucking right we do," Dave says. "What's holding you up?"

I pick up the copy of Leeds Lite and hold it in front of my face, blocking him out, pretending to study it. I try not to look at my photograph. I stare at the words underneath until they blur. When I first started writing, I used to read newspapers and steal lines from them. Bad headlines. *Cat Caught In Tree. Triple Jump Disaster.* Once, I could even have got a song out of a crap review. I was a magpie, joyful, lifting things and hoarding them, jumbling them up. I don't know why I can't see the same patterns any more. Sometimes, I think I used to find it easier to say things when I was trying not to.

He pulls the magazine down, ripping it slightly and stares at me, like he's going to nut me or kiss me.

"What the fuck is going on with you?"

I can still see the couple in my peripheral vision, eating and eating and eating. I feel nauseous again. I try to stand up, but the room begins to swim, softly out of focus and I sit down abruptly. I am faintly aware of Dave saying my name.

"Lorna. Look at me."

I do. I wish I hadn't. "What?"

"Are you alright?"

I say nothing. He doesn't care anyway. None of them does, as long as I keep the songs coming, as long as I turn up with lyrics they can riff off and get wrong and break up.

Instead, I ask him, "Have you spoken to Simon since the gig?"

"Oh yeah," he laughs. "I took him flowers yesterday. We had a cup of tea and swapped notes about Carla. We're going to a spa next week."

"You should call him."

"I don't have anything left to say to that dickhead." He spits out the word, but I still find it comical.

"Sort it out," I say. "For the sake of the band."

"If I find out he's texted Carla again, I'll stick his drumsticks up his tight little arse."

I nod sagely. "I'm glad you're working things out."

"I've never fucking trusted him. Not since the tour."

It wasn't a tour. It was two nights in London, playing pubs in Camden and Islington. I don't want to think about the harsh blue lights and backstage vodka, Carla and Simon groping in the back of the van while Dave was half passed-out in the front, all of us trying to ignore it. I've never got on with Carla. She's got blonde, corkscrew curls and fleshy shoulders. She walks like somebody who actually likes herself. On the last night, I watched her stick a needle in Dave's arm through the door of the crap B&B we'd treated ourselves to. I watched his whole body soften and her smile creasing her face, looking at him like she loved him. I've never told Dave that I saw.

"You could have done a better job last week. Knocked him out or something."

"Next time I will."

I close my eyes. Somewhere, in the empty pit of my stomach, I know there won't be a next time. I smile at him and squeeze his arm. He does not see me. I glance back at the photo, the picture taken by someone who didn't see me either, just my outline and my hair, my shadow across the stage. I don't want them to see me. I want to be a voice. I choose dresses and boots the colour of the stage and curtains. My hair is getting darker by design.

"Give that here," says Dave, flicking through the pages manically. He stops on a spread about the Arctic Monkeys playing a secret gig at the Brudenell. He holds it aloft. "I look like him, don't you reckon?"

"Alex Turner on acid."

"Carla reckons I do." He pouts and takes his hat off. "Fuck me, I'm famous."

I can't write a song about anything I hear or see because I don't find anything funny any more. Even Dave's gurn, even his wayward eyebrows.

"I'm getting a pie," he pushes his chair back and almost tips it over. "You want anything?"

I shake my head.

The room starts getting blurry then. Like a stage before the lights come up. I hold on to the arms of my chair.

I don't know how long I'm out for. When I come round, Dave has left me. There's a napkin folded over on the table in front of me with a biro scrawl right across it, in capitals, underlined.

Sort yourself out.

Next to it, he's left me the bill for a single steak and ale pie.

MICHAEL

I think it was Tuesday. Tuesday, maybe, and raining. You know, those afternoons when it seems like midnight at 4pm and you want to go into a pub, an old man's pub, and sit in the snug? Look, do I even know you? I mean did we meet before this? OK. And you remember that, do you, because its your job to remember everything and wear your collar buttoned up like that, like...?

I'm sorry. Yeah, I'll go back to the beginning. Can I ask you something first though? I mean, have you ever thought about it yourself? Seriously? Because don't you think if you haven't thought about it you might not be in the right line of work? Sorry. Have I offended you? I mean isn't it a bit like being a dairy farmer and never drinking a pint of milk? Or like being a vegetarian butcher? Or, I don't know, being a car mechanic who never learned to drive?

Well, what do you think? Do I actually look like the kind of guy who would? Did you know that its most common, statistically I mean? Our age group. You're the same age as me aren't you? So I guess it's likely, isn't it... even if I've never got as far as planning anything I must have had those thoughts at least once or twice. Statistically. Right. But listen - don't you think talking about it in the abstract is a bit patronising? Like it's pretending to understand when you don't. Like looking at the stars from your back garden every night and assuming you know what it's like to go into space.

Do you think you can tell by looking at someone? If I said that I'd be able to tell if I'd seen her in the street before, would you believe me? Hindsight. Maybe. Is there some special reason you want to know about her anyway? Has this come from higher up? It seems like more than curiosity from where I'm standing. Have they given you a woman? Is that what this is about? And you expect me to just tell you everything like all the things we talked about and how her hair fell across her face and what she drank and what it said in her file and all the preferences she gave and...

Do you remember all of your jobs? Right. And you think I'm any different? Oh, you don't buy it. You think because they're women I take some...special interest. So, what...you're implying I get too attached? No? So if she *was* my client would it make you feel better if I said I was kinder to her than the others? Depends what you mean by kindness. I mean is it kinder to cut someone's life support if they're unconscious or is it kinder to try and bring them round forever?

Don't you ever ask yourself things like that, though? Do you think people have the right to always get what they want? I mean, do you think it makes it easier if they don't have a family? Well, that depends on how you define society. I mean, where do you draw the line? Sometimes I wonder... well, it doesn't matter. Just... whether we're so... I keep thinking about this film, just this film about a mechanic in Germany who made parts and they just seemed like parts like made to specifications for vehicles and he made them and one day he found out the cargo was humans and they were going... they were being taken away... Do you know it? I can't remember the name.

Anyhow, what was I telling you about her? Did I say that it was raining for hours and when she arrived she was soaked? Look, do you actually want to know about her or not?

GERRY

1. I never edit. Editing is like fucking someone until they come and then apologising.

2. Should I have said 'making love'?

3. I woke up on the floor and Chairman was on the bed, wheezing. Chairman Miaow. Best I could do at the time. I never thought I'd have a cat. Passive-aggressive fuckers at best, psychopaths at worst, climbing the curtains and shitting in secret. But Chairman turned up when she was a kitten and I liked her style - slinky, devious to a point. Anyway. She was in the middle of the bed and I was on my side down below the radiator with a head like a goldfish bowl. Like a shark in a goldfish bowl. Or a shark in a bag, one of those plastic bags you used to get at the fair. Fairground hammerhead.

4. This is how it goes, lately. I get a thought and I chase it down and I net the fucker, over and over, until I'm under the net and fighting with it. Am I making myself clear? I've had two pieces sent back this month, first time in ten years. *We think the writing may be slightly too elaborate for the client's needs.* Or *you may want to reconsider the phrasing of 'my life was as a large as a giraffe, its neck was poking through the bathroom window.'* The first time, I didn't reply. The second time, I sent them an acrostic poem that spelled 'FUCK YOU' down the side.

5. Editing is like killing a man and then firing a bullet into his lifeless corpse.

6. I haven't always known I was a poet. What is it they say? Hiding your light under a bus shelter. People make assumptions. Shaved head. Busting out of my shirt. Last week, I went to the bar at The

Emperor and read the Penguin Classic Yevtushenko. There were two lasses doing Jaegerbombs, one of them almost falling off her stool and I just lowered the book and looked over the top at them for a minute, like this. When they carried on, I walked between them, picked up one of the empties and brought it down on the bar. One of them got glass lodged in her arm.

7. How do you know Shakespeare didn't look like a rugby league player?

8. I like John Donne and I like Tarantino. That's a good mix. Innovative. I'm a bit like both of them, but I've got Quentin's eye. You have to be careful though. Violence only works when it's unpredictable. You can't be anticipating it all the time. I like my poetry to take someone's coat and then take their fingers off.

9. If you really want to scare someone, do it the other way round. Fingers, then coat.

10. On the other hand, you might prefer to make them live in a constant state of dread.

11. There's this lad I know who lives like that. Don. Good kid, terrible writer. I met him in the bogs at Temple Bar. He had stage fright at the urinal. Even that first time, I knew he'd take to the job. Everything he says is an apology and he's got one of those thin mouths, lips like a line drawn under a shopping list.

12. Last week, I went to an open mic night in the Northern Quarter. My first. Poetry virgin. I was late and the sign-up sheet was already full, there was a skinny guy with a curled moustache guarding it. He looked bored, so I picked the paper up off the table and rolled it into a tight cigar shape and then I dropped it into his pint of cider. He said nothing. I took another piece of paper from the table and

wrote my name in capitals across the top. In the end, I left before my turn anyway. There was a woman who read with her back to the audience, both her hands in the air like she was conducting an orchestra. Everything was about transformation. Butterflies. A chrysalis. There was a teenager whose face turned red the angrier he got. Then there was the bloke who threw glitter across the first row. I've still got some on my jeans. I don't like being touched, not even by crap confetti. It had been in his pocket, inside his clothes. I moved on to The Castle instead and read my poem aloud there to Irish Kevin across the bar - he never took his eyes from mine.

13. Editing is like sitting in someone's house with your coat on and then taking it off just before you leave. Underneath, you're topless.

14. If I did have an editor though, I'd want someone like Gordon Lish. Someone who'd cut out all the bullshit. Maybe just leave me with the title. All or nothing. I bet you didn't think I'd read Raymond Carver, did you? They don't have editors like Lish at my place. I work for amateurs in polyester suits.

15. The greatest compliment you can give someone is a short obituary.

16. My worst ever job was a woman from Preston who had lived alone for ten years. One sister she hadn't spoken to since they were teenagers. It said on her file she had been a chess champion, played games from a distance with people she'd never met. Postal chess. It took me ages to get my head round that. I imagined them sending the pieces back and forth. Knights and rooks in envelopes. Apparently, it's all done on paper. I couldn't get inside her head. I tried imagining her thinking out the moves, maybe sketching them in the air with a pencil, but I couldn't picture it. Couldn't see inside anything she might have loved. I kept the note brief in the end. *Check mate.*

17. Mark Twain saw his own obituary. Hemingway too. He put a scrapbook together of all the reports of his death and read them after breakfast every morning with a glass of champagne.

18. Jo DiMaggio. Samuel Taylor Coleridge. Pope John Paul II.

19. I don't write obituaries, I write apologies. *I wish to be excused from my life.* Obituaries are the one noble art. A poem's like an obituary. A novel's like a suicide note. Some novels, you just wish they'd hurry up and get on with it.

20. When I was a kid, I used to climb pylons with my friend Mick. We were inspired by those videos at school, the ones where you see a boy clambering up after his kite, getting fried somewhere near the top and plummeting down to the ground. I used to let Mick go first. Sometimes, up high, I'd feel like jumping off. It was overwhelming, a kind of tight pull, like there was a wire from my stomach to the ground. I didn't want to die but I didn't really care if I did either. Death as an aside. One time when I felt like that, I wound my hand round Mick's jumper instead, pulling the fabric at the back of his neck. I told him I was going to drop him. Asked him what his last words were going to be. He was white in the face, shaking. The dumb bastard couldn't even say anything.

21. Editing is like knocking someone out cold and realising you should have knocked yourself out instead.

22. You haven't lived until you've stared in the mirror and punched yourself in the face, just to see what it feels like.

KATHY

I only visited Michael at his house once - that was all that was required of me. It was the end of summer and the trees that stooped over the approach from the station were a premature gold. The track climbed severely up the hill, potholed, pitted with stones. I was wearing my work shoes and my feet were chilled by the puddles. The incline made me pause for breath. It was dusk, or close to it and the rain had started to insist. When I stopped where the leaves were densest for shelter, the foliage crackled above me and a group of birds took off with a sound I thought for a moment was my own. I realised how long it had been since I had spoken to anyone. I stood, letting the silence and my heartbeat settle.

It was a small cottage, the rock outcrop behind it overshadowing the house, but it seemed to loom over the approach. I noticed a mountain bike propped by the front door, mud spattered up the frame and made a note to log it in my report. *House in remote location, evidence of outdoor interests.*

I had to knock three times. I listened for the pause in between, like counting after thunder. Across the valley, a bull was lowing. I was about to turn around when I saw his shadow behind the frosted window. When he opened the door, his dark hair was damp and tousled. He must have just got out of the shower. I felt faintly uncomfortable, but I didn't let it show. One mustn't.

"You must be Kathy," he held out a hand, shook mine too firmly. "I hope you found the place okay."

"May I come in?" My hair was clinging to my face. I went to take my shoes off, but he waved his arm genially.

"Make yourself at home."

The living room was purposeful. Bookshelf. Television. Oak cabinet with three bottles of single malt whisky on top. I should have noted that but I didn't. I watched him fumbling to clear a space on the threadbare settee. He was unshaven, but there was a precision about him and his movement that didn't match the room. There were no curtains, but it was very dark and I imagined it was like this at all times of day. As I sat down, I straightened my skirt.

"Towel?" he said, holding one out to me. "For your hair?"

I shook my head, and again at the offer of tea. "I won't keep you long, Mr..."

He noticed me checking the file. "Singer. Take as long as you like, Kathy."

The way he sat was disarming. Comfortable. A good sign. I reminded myself this was his territory, you can't read too much into it. Sometimes, I meet them in city coffee shops, bars, the kinds of places the job might take them. I watch how they order their drink, how well they blend in.

"I must say, I don't think I've ever been somewhere quite so... remote, before."

"It was my dad's old place. I came to clear it out and I ended up staying. It suits me. The back garden isn't so bad for a climber."

I laughed. "Quite." I hadn't noticed the tightly-wound blue rope by the hearth. I glanced at him, the hardness of his ridged arms. "As I say, this won't be an unduly long interview. Just a few routine questions and an opportunity for you to ask me anything you'd like to about the role."

"I don't think I have any questions, Kathy."

I'll admit I was surprised by that. They usually have a whole list. Nervous. I smiled, nodded. There was one framed pictured above the hearth. A photograph of a ridge cloaked in snow, a figure in an orange helmet, climbing, head tilted downwards so it was impossible to tell if it was a man or a woman. Oblivious to the camera. I glimpsed back at Michael, assessing his shape.

Before I started with *Exire*, when I was a sports psychologist in the States, I worked with a free climber from Colorado, a religious tee-totaller who rose to fame in the 1990s for a series of daring solos in Yosemite and Western Canada. Rob DeLuca. His full name was Roberto. He was a wiry Italian who moved awkwardly everywhere except the rock face. Michael was nothing like him with his confident, easy manner and open face; but as I watched him steeling his hands, then smoothing down his jeans, touching his ear almost instinctively - a gesture that seemed to comfort him - I kept thinking of Roberto's camper van in the parking lot he lived in, somewhere on the outskirts of Yosemite National Park. Whenever I arrived, he'd twitch the curtains of the van, making sure it wasn't the Rangers. I never became comfortable in his company. Nor was I sure I could help him much, not when it came down to it. What he wanted was what he already had. He was just afraid of it. Sometimes, in our sessions, something would pass across his face like a shadow over granite.

Michael seemed expectant; he sat so his body faced mine. I cleared my throat. "As you'll have been informed by my colleague Jane, your performance on the X8 test was excellent, a very high score indeed. This visit is really just a follow up and a chance to make sure we're right for you as well as vice versa."

You can't always infer too much from the tests. Some people think they're more detached than they are. Abstract pain, that's one thing. But Michael was a climber. I thought of Roberto, the diagrams and sketches that papered the walls of his van. Planning. Scoping out the moves in order to execute them. Practical and efficient.

"If you'll forgive me," I said. "I do need to ask you a few things, as a formality."

"Of course."

I bent to retrieve my iPad from my satchel and as I stooped, there was a papery thud against the window. I flinched, gripping the arm of the sofa. It was a black bird, oily feathers, the size of a crow. It hit the glass and fell. Michael let out a hoarse laugh and I recovered myself.

"Starlings. I had one in the chimney last week."

It had looked bigger. I glanced at the unlit fireplace and thought of the chimney flue, imagined the shape of something battering around in there, like a hand, flailing. I laughed too, a giddy kind of sound. I was thinking of a Ted Hughes poem we read at school when I was a child. Something about starlings. No. *Terrifying are the thrushes on the lawn, // more coiled steel than living.* Not a starling at all.

"Well, if you're ready, Mr Singer."

"Michael, please."

"Michael. The first question is of a rather personal nature, I'm afraid. I hope you won't find it unduly intrusive. I'd like you to begin by telling me about some of your closest relationships."

No girlfriend. One sibling in Australia. His parents both dead. He was ideal. As he spoke, I found myself looking through the open door to the hallway, the stairwell, imagining the disorder of his room. I wondered if he ever had company at all, company of that kind I mean. I was alarmed by this, hoping the thought didn't show. I had the strange sensation of watching my own body from above, of being high over the cottage looking down, the roof lifted off so I could see his bed, the sparse bathroom with its old fashioned basin, the dark rectangle of the chimney, the live things inside it. I remembered a film I'd watched of Roberto, soloing The Nose on El Capitan, the shots taken from a helicopter, the spider-like movements he made up the face, a surface that - from that distance - seemed to look like sand. I still have recordings of all his climbs, somewhere. At first, they were research, looking for the clues in his body, the way he moved, but soon I began to find their sequences comforting. The inevitability of it, the point where he'd step over the top and the camera would come in for a close-up.

"Is that all you need?"

"Yes, thank you." I looked down at the screen. I had failed to enter a score in any of the boxes. I could do it later, on the train. "That's extremely thorough. We'll be in touch if we need any more information. But you mustn't hesitate to contact us either if..."

"I won't change my mind."

"...if you have any questions for us."

He stood up and I followed him. Now that our conversation was over, his ease had calcified into something else. He seemed on edge, eager for me to be gone. I picked up my jacket from the arm of the chair. In the doorway, I paused and turned back.

"Michael, I... I'm not at liberty to give details but it seems likely that your first assignment, your first client seems likely to be... I mean... They're likely to give someone like you a challenge."

A challenge. That was how Roberto used to describe his routes. He didn't use the word 'project' like other climbers. It was always *my next challenge, the challenge of the Dawn Wall, the challenge I've set for myself.*

"Excellent." His face betrayed nothing. "I'd like to be pushed."

I was holding on to the door handle.

"I just wanted you to be aware. Whilst the majority of our clients are male, we do have requests from women. You might be asked..."

"Of course."

I felt slightly foolish, as if I'd patronised him. I pulled my coat around me.

Roberto was killed in a base-jumping accident in Western Australia. His parachute failed to open. There was a documentary on the news, late at night, but I discovered the programme quite by chance. I read his obituaries, of course. They even contacted me for a magazine, one of the glossy, high-end American publications. An insight into his state of mind, what drove him. I couldn't give them anything.

Michael closed the door behind me. I began to hurry down the track, realising it would be prudent to try and catch an earlier train if I could, leave enough time for my connection. I had the sensation of being watched. When I looked back over my shoulder, the lights in the cottage were bright against the hillside, which seemed to go on forever.

DON

The Optimist and The Pessimist are in a pub where the landlord hates customers. Eastenders plays on the miniature corner TV with subtitles no-one has been able to switch off. The barman is invisible behind a copy of *OK!*. The Optimist stands at the bar and coughs politely for exactly three and a half minutes while The Pessimist sits at a back table, tearing a beer mat into squares and pushing the bits together.

The Optimist carries two pints of Peroni without spilling a drop. It is a week and a day since The Optimist sent The Pessimist a Facebook message. HEY! it said. Then, moments later: LONG TIME NO SEE!!! DON'T KNOW WHY I'M USING CAPITALS - LOL. FANCY A PINT? There were a pair of kisses at the end, in lower case. When The Pessimist didn't reply, The Optimist shared a photograph on The Pessimist's wall of the Student Union Freshers' pyjama party, The Pessimist in a checked flannel shirt and The Optimist naked from the waist up. THROWBACK THURSDAY! it said underneath, with a smiley face. Then, a status update: *Good friends are like stars: you don't always have to see them to know they're there!!!*

The pub jukebox is playing Careless Whisper.

"Isn't this great?" says The Optimist. "I can't believe the tap room's hardly changed in twenty years!"

The Pessimist asks The Optimist a series of rehearsed questions and downs half a pint while The Optimist answers. They have determined that they live ten minutes away from each other when the traffic is good, which The Pessimist knows is seldom.

The Optimist has had a challenging few years but is practicing Tai

Chi these days, which is wonderful for the core. The Optimist's son was diagnosed with a serious condition at the age of two and requires around-the-clock supervision. The Optimist's marriage is good in the circumstances because many couples The Optimist has met with similar responsibilities split up. The Optimist published a paper in The Journal of Social Anthropology shortly after graduating, but hasn't been able to write since. However, The Optimist is a voracious reader! The Optimist can get through five books in a good week!

The Pessimist has had a moderately successful career in the publishing industry, rising to a middle management position and avoiding redundancy when the company downsized. The Pessimist has a pebbledash cottage in North West Scotland and holidays there twice a year, though The Pessimist is concerned about the property market.

The Optimist observes that The Pessimist's glass is half-full while The Optimist's is almost empty. The Optimist suggests they get shots of sambuca. "My treat," says The Optimist, but The Pessimist has a mild intolerance to aniseed. The Pessimist drinks a bottle of Isla Negra most nights after work, standing up in the kitchen under a flickering spot light, but isn't used to pints and has the strong urge to pee.

While they talk, The Optimist reaches across the table to touch The Pessimist on the arm from time to time and The Pessimist doesn't reciprocate. The Optimist has very tanned, taut forearms. The Optimist finds it difficult to fit workouts around caring responsibilities, but The Optimist discovered the 5-2 diet a few years ago and lost over three stone. The Pessimist has a higher than average metabolism but binges on supermarket cookies jewelled with white chocolate chips and individually packaged protein bars designed for people who do power lifting. The Pessimist has never seen the point of joining a gym when the membership fees are so high.

The Pessimist stumbles out for a piss, knocking the table and The Optimist goes for more pints.

The landlord says the lager is off and they'll have to have John Smith's or Strongbow. Which does The Optimist prefer?

"Surprise me!" says The Optimist, letting him keep the change.

The Pessimist is spending a long time in the toilets, so The Optimist uses the opportunity to text a mutual friend and comment on the low level sexual tension that has existed between The Pessimist and The Optimist since they met in Halls.

STILL HOT! says The Optimist, with a winking emoticon.

After their fourth pint, The Optimist makes a series of points about independent schools that The Pessimist disagrees with on principle. The Optimist intends to have a larger family and The Optimist would like to send them to St Peter's. The Pessimist has no children. The Optimist also founded a charity for homeless people in South Croydon. The Pessimist thinks it is difficult to be sure that cash donations won't be spent on alcohol.

The Pessimist agrees to a shot of tequila with lemon and salt and another pint. The Optimist knows some brilliant drinking games, does The Pessimist remember King's Cup and how Gordon from Slough had to down a whole measuring jug full of WKD and white wine? The Optimist brushes The Pessimist's knee under the table and The Pessimist moves away slightly.

The Pessimist is speaking in sentences that aren't properly connected. Sometimes, The Pessimist murmurs to someone invisible off to the right. The Optimist is very animated. The Optimist has so many plans for the next ten years! There's a brilliant local co-operative that has been raising funds for The Optimist's son to go to Disneyland. The Optimist has also been selling cannabis on the side and it has been amazingly lucrative. The Optimist learned Spanish through a CD.

The Pessimist attends weekly therapy sessions but the therapist is too young to understand. Pills, says The Pessimist. The Pessimist was too scared to go through with it. The Optimist has suffered from depression in the past but found that a diet high in B-vitamins and iron was a tremendous help. Since The Optimist has seen how much their son has suffered, The Optimist has learned the value of living in the present. Does The Pessimist realise that - really - we've all won the lottery just by being born in the UK? The Optimist knows someone really great The Pessimist should talk to.

The Pessimist staggers towards the toilets. The Optimist sends another message:

FLIRTY BANTER! says The Optimist with two winky faces.

The landlord has turned the strip lights off above the bar. The Optimist reaches into a pocket and gets out a green capsule and breaks it into The Pessimist's drink so that the powder sighs into the middle of the glass. The Optimist gives the cider a good stir with a straw, takes the straw out, bends and pockets it.

"Drink up," says The Optimist when The Pessimist comes back. "Cheers!"

They clink glasses. The Pessimist has never really liked cider. There's a blunt, chemical taste to most brands. But The Pessimist will drink anything. Soon, The Pessimist feels more relaxed. The Pessimist's chair is the centre of a soft-boiled egg. The Pessimist is having difficulty walking in a straight line, but The Optimist has strong shoulders from all the Tai Chi. The Optimist steers The Pessimist out onto the street where the all-night takeaway blinks pale.

The Optimist is staying in a Premier Inn in town tonight and The Pessimist is in no fit state to go home. The Optimist is on the 10th floor and, even through the fog, the city below is brilliant with amber, can't The Pessimist see? The Optimist points out the red buses and how they all have strips of white on the roofs, but The Pessimist can't focus on them.

"Magic!" says The Optimist.

The Optimist and The Pessimist fuck quietly with The Pessimist underneath clinging on to the bed. There are two different types of pillow available in the room and if you need more you only have to ask. The Pessimist is sick and doesn't quite make it to the bathroom, but The Optimist cleans it with a t-shirt. In the dark, The Optimist holds on to The Pessimist very tightly and strokes The Pessimist's hair. The Pessimist is drifting in and out of consciousness, breathing raggedly and The Optimist tries to wake The Pessimist up, pressing hard into the Pessimist's back.

"I just feel so close to you," says The Optimist. Outside, the cars pass without stopping.

*

I showed that story to Gerry.

"Guess which one is me?" I said.

Gerry said I could lose everything apart from the last paragraph.

LORNA

I sit down to write a song. I haven't written for months and I'm here, I'm doing it. The words are on the tip of my tongue. But they're the wrong words. And it isn't a song. I'm writing a story and it is mine.

It is a large dark room, empty except for one chair and, across the walls, the city, stretched upside down. I see blue and white first, in soft focus. Then a red bus, travelling on its roof. A group of shoppers standing on their heads. L. shows it all to me with the half-glee of a child. His face always holds something childlike, even though he must be in his late forties. Unshaven, with a clutch of black hair, his checked shirt unbuttoned to show the greyer hairs on his chest. But I'm not looking at him like that. I stare at the spread-out, upended street. The tipped-up shops and pubs. The sky where the floor should be.

I've never really understood the principles of camera obscura. I suppose it captures something of the way we see the world first, before the brain turns it around. Something to do with light passing through a small gap or pinhole, how it projects an image of the surroundings, rotated 180 degrees. How, as the pinhole gets smaller, the image gets larger but the projection becomes dimmer. I can register all these facts in the abstract, but I can't relate them to that attic room, that banner of the city, the moving kaleidoscope of it all. L.'s face with the street flickering over it.

I stop. I need to begin somewhere else. I need to go backwards:

The first time I met L. in his studio, he showed me the upstairs room, the strange palette of the walls. He smoked skinny roll ups, breathed smoke theatrically and talked about light and the eye.

Once I got used to seeing the city upside down, I noticed how things looked together. The buildings hung down like icicles. Or perhaps it was more like fruit on a tree. Something about them made me think of the caves I once saw in Pileta, rocks hanging from the roof of the cave like strange teeth. I started to watch it as if it was a film. A woman and a man walking upside down and arm in arm along the pavement, the improbability of her hat, clinging to her head. Two men opening the back doors of a van, unloading it, the cargo set down where you expected sky. It felt like watching a nativity at first, or a scene in a snowglobe. I couldn't imagine it all happening the right way up, just outside the window. Once you get used to something, you can't imagine looking differently.

I'm still not getting it right. I start again. There are things I don't want to say. I cross through the page and turn over:

"You can undress behind the screen."

I did it very slowly, afraid to move out into the bright room. There was something bizarre in the modesty of stepping out of my dress behind cover when he was going to see me naked but, somehow, it felt like an important ritual, a mark of respect. All that summer, I'd change behind the screen. Arrange my shoes. Fold my tights and underwear on top of them. Walk carefully across the dirty floorboards, the soles of my feet blackening straight away.

I stood in front of the screen, between the pinhole and the screen and let the street arrange itself across me. I was lit by the upside-down city. It was a bit like a moving tattoo. I couldn't really tell what I looked like except for what L. told me – once, a bicycle swam past slowly, moving across my stomach and he laughed out loud. He took picture after picture. Sometimes I turned my back to the camera, sometimes I stood side on. He'd murmur "beautiful" or "lovely" under his breath. At first, I was aware of my body – the curve of my belly that I hated so much, my skinny chest and my broad shoulders. I've never been able to stand my shape. I always wanted to fold myself away as quickly as possible. Having someone look at all of me was the most unnerving thing I could imagine. But at some point that morning, I stopped thinking about my own skin and only noticed the light. Or I began to watch L., kneeling or crouching, the way his body seemed to crowd behind the lens of the camera.

I made excuses to go more and more often. We'd sit in front of L.'s cluttered desk, avalanched with sketches and notes and flyers for exhibitions, and he'd chain smoke and we'd talk about art and things that made us feel alive. His obsession with light, how it came from long walks home in the pitch black when he was a student. A couple of times, he mentioned his family and I tried to imagine his house under the leafy canopy of the suburbs, imagined walking past at night and seeing them silhouetted in the kitchen, distant behind glass and shared happiness. Mostly, though, we spoke through art. I'd tell him about a song I loved or an idea that captured my imagination; he'd mention something visual that it reminded him of. Cy Twombly. Derek Mahon's 'Leaves'. Cornelia Parker. Soon, I was going round after work as well. The camera obscura looked even more striking at dusk when you could see street lights and traffic lights in it, the gold rectangles of the pub and apartment windows.

Around the same time, I started modelling for life drawing classes at the University. I wanted to do it because of how much the idea terrified me. Posing in front of a group of architecture students, my body tilted or twisted, my arms above my head, I felt strangely calm and thoughtful. There was something hushed and respectful about the atmosphere of the life drawing class. Standing above a dozen people sketching, working out which poses to do, I had space to think. At first, I worried about them judging me, noticing my awkward shape, the cellulite on my legs or my weird, muscular back. I obsessed about waxing and shaving and worried about sweating under the lights. But in the silence of the room, I relaxed into every pose. I felt *more like a tree or a stretch of moving water than a person. I could even view the students' pictures afterwards with a kind of detached approval. The life drawing classes gave me a temporary comfort in my own skin. Once, a spider dropped from the ceiling and landed on my shoulder while I was modelling and I just let it run down my torso.*

I am leaving things out. What I'm afraid to say is this:

I don't know when I started imagining L. in corners of the city where he wouldn't be. Cycling down the narrow streets near The Alma. Reading in cafes on Ash Road. I didn't mean to catch glimpses of him in places he wasn't, but I did. Once, I did really see him on a stretch of road near my house. He was with his wife and they were teaching their kids to cycle along the quiet pavement. They had stabilisers and shiny cycling helmets. He saw me and pretended he hadn't. And I did the same.

One lunchtime at work, it was a stifling, muggy kind of day, the kind where you want it to rain to clear the air. I'd been up since dawn, agitated and wired on black coffee. I'd had an argument with my boyfriend, something about his ex coming back to town. I spent my lunch hour snapping at him down the phone and walking aimlessly round the Botanical gardens, looking at strange orange flowers shaped a bit like birds. Then I walked round to the studio to see if the door was ajar.

I never felt comfortable telling L. much about my personal life or my own problems. It was easier following tangents about art. Or talking through the camera obscura, noticing things together. A workman painting a sign white. The birds that weren't so much landing as falling. A small, tawny dog.

"Would you like me to give you a head massage?"

L. got me to sit on the floor on a piece of cardboard in front of the camera obscura. He sat on a wooden stool behind me so that I was leaning back on his knees, or slightly between his knees. It was raining in the upside down street, the drops were rising towards the pavement sky. Apart from weather, the road was near-deserted for once, just the occasional car with headlights on, or the squeal of a bike. He began to touch my hair. His fingers were moving in circles round and round my scalp, very slowly and gently at first. I closed my eyes and let my head fall heavy in his hands. Soon, it felt like he was cradling my whole face. Close up, I could smell him, a mix of tobacco and that singular way that someone's skin seems perfumed when you're that near to them. I'd been holding my back quite straight but as he massaged my head, I let myself relax against his legs.

I might have been there for hours. I could make out the hiss of traffic outside and imagined everything going past in the camera obscura. At some point, I became aware of L. reaching down to unbutton my blouse, then slipping it over my shoulders, reaching down to unhook my bra. I stiffened and almost froze. I could feel my heartbeat loud in my ribcage. His hands moved down over my shoulders, cupping them and then gripping them. He massaged my back, my neck and my stomach, kneading my skin. I didn't open my eyes. Sometimes his fingers almost brushed my nipples, but he never touched them. His hands moved in circles down to the waistband of my black jeans, but he never unbuttoned them. He was breathing deeply and slowly, the way people do when they're asleep. I didn't dare move. I let him mould my body. In fact, I almost imagined he was re-sculpting it, like clay.

At some point, as easily as he'd started to touch me, he cleared his throat and stopped. Pulling my bra and blouse on, I couldn't look him in the eye or think of much to say when I left. He looked at the camera obscura playing out its shapes on the wall. I walked out into the rain.

I sit and stare down at the page for a long time. I need to finish this:

All that summer, he never kissed me, but he held his face close to mine. He never undressed, but he pressed my face against his shirt. He never tried to fuck me. He just touched me, all over my skin, without saying anything, over and over and over and over. And we never spoke about it. Every night, I went home and couldn't sleep. I stayed up, sitting behind a desk I'd rescued from a charity shop, watching the lights go off one by one in a house on Bateman Street. I'd walk to work in the mornings and not remember getting there. And day after day, I went to model for the life drawing class. Or I sat or lay on the floor and let him undress me, detached and tender. I let him touch me with an intimacy I couldn't name. I just let it happen.

I don't know when I started to resent L. and the control he had over my body, whether touching my skin or directing me to stand a certain way in one of his classes. I started to view myself as if from above. Even my own hands seemed strange when I looked down at them. When I thought of myself, it was like thinking about a person you might see in the corner of someone else's photograph, caught, held, carrying on doing what they were doing, away from the lens. Suddenly and deliberately, I applied for a job somewhere else, north west. On the day I was due to move north, L. asked me to come round. He was cheerful and jovial. Last thing, he handed me a slim brown envelope. As I walked down the stairs for the last time, I was breathless, imagining a letter, a goodbye or a declaration of some kind. It was just a photograph of me, turning away from the camera, my body lit blue and unfamiliar, the tattoo on my back giving me away. I sealed the envelope and set off along Bridge Street, the same street held in the camera obscura. From the room above, he might have watched me leave, upside down.

GERRY

23. Writing, on the other hand, that's like skinny-dipping in a moonlit lake while some fucker runs off with your clothes.

24. I used to make up stories when I was a kid and take them to my mum, but she was pissed and didn't know what to do with them. Once, she spilled wine on one and turned it sideways and held it up to the light sideways and stared through it, like stained glass. She started crying. That was when I knew she couldn't read.

25. All you care about is the cold lake, so cold you can feel all the bones in your body. You walk home stark bollock naked and you don't care.

26. The wankers in the office sent me to see a therapist last week. Bald bastard in glasses, a room that smelled of fruit. I had fun with him. Made up some shit about my dad kicking the doors in to get to me, how I'd shake when I heard his footsteps up the stairs. He held his knees and nodded very slowly. He didn't make any notes.

27. Writing is like crossing the motorway in snow for the hell of it. Feeling like you're in a computer game. Timing it so the cars get a bit too close.

28. I never saw my dad. Only his photo in the spare room.

29. Sometimes, you feel like a car could just hit you and pass straight through, the way the snow hits you and sinks into your collar and the back of your coat.

30. I wrote that down, then I decided it was pretentious. Snow. Too fucking predictable.

31. I told baldy my dad was in a gang. Made him sound like one of the Kray twins. The best bit was watching him trying not to look shocked while I talked about torture, about slicing a man's fingerprints off his hands. The room was painted in beige and pale blue and there was something beige about baldy too.

32. *Boredom*, I said. *Mostly I'm so bored I could eat myself* [1] and he raised his eyebrows. It's a quotation from a poem, but he didn't get it.

33. I started on Bukowski next. I said *there's a bluebird in my heart that wants to get out but I'm too tough for him.*

34. Writing is like stealing a job lot from the supermarket - steaks and bacon and cheese and small electronics - then getting home and wondering how you're going to sell them all off.

35. If there is a bluebird in my heart, Chairman Miaow would probably eat the fucker.

36. *How does it feel? asked the therapist, is the bird singing?*

37. I nodded and I clenched my fists, like this.

38. Writing is like breaking into someone else's house at 1am. You've been watching the place for weeks, you know exactly what time the lights go out and you're in now, keeping very quiet. Upstairs, they're sound asleep. It's a big house and there are plasma screen tellies, an iPad propped on one of the kitchen work surfaces. You know you should work quickly and get the fuck out, but instead you're looking at the photos on the hall table. This girl standing next to a horse with her hair falling over one shoulder. You walk quietly through all the rooms. You imagine sitting in the grey, matching armchairs with a glass of chilled wine in one hand. Then, you just leave, just get the Hell out of there and close the door behind you.

1. Carol Ann Duffy, *Stealing*.

39. When you get down the road, you realise you pocketed the girl's photograph, but you don't remember doing it.

40. *Does the bird have a name?* asked the therapist. I looked at him and nodded with my jaw set. *Barry*, I said with a straight face. *Barry Manilow.* He wrote something down in his little notebook then.

41. When mum's boyfriend Karl moved in, I was already hanging about at the rec more than I was home anyway. He did me a favour. I remember his pissy little eyes, so brown you could hardly make out the pupils. When he got me against the wall, I could see them contract, like he was trying to pull me in. I could have decked him but I never did. He didn't lay a finger on her; it was just me he hated. I shoved some things in a hold-all - toothbrush, pants, jumpers, copy of *On The Road* - and I never looked back, not even when I could hear mum in the kitchen.

42. Writing is like dealing heroin. To know if it's any good, you have to take a hit yourself.

43. When I was 18, I was pretty good at dealing really. I never got a habit. When I heard about *Exire*, it seemed like the same thing: peddling something you'd only flirt with yourself.

44. Then again, writing is like a habit you never meant to get.

45. Never trust anyone who isn't addicted to something.

MASON

The presenter has a moustache as thin as a biro line. I think it might be drawn on. I think his whole face might be a drawing, actually. I'm staring at him, trying to work out if it's true that his whole waist is on the size of my right arm, which is what it looks like. Even his tie is skinny. His slides stopped working half an hour ago and the PowerPoint is frozen on an image of a man in a white shirt and braces, two other men stooping towards him and fixing something to his arms.

"So they're in the lab now. They draw straws to decide who will play each role. But it's a fix, naturally it's a fix. So the 'learner' is always played by a confederate, someone in on the whole thing. And there's this 'experimenter' in a grey lab coat, but he's an actor, he's just an actor, he doesn't need to do much. They sit them in two different rooms and they strap the learner to a chair with electrodes attached to him. Is this all clear so far? It would be better if the images had..."

I yawn without covering my mouth. I get my phone out of my pocket and press refresh on my emails. A report from Kathy, the needy, anorexic psychologist about her latest profile for employment interview. A message in capitals from David about the writer on his team he's having trouble with: THINKS HE'S WRITING FUCKING POETRY. CALLED LAST DRAFT 'MISSIVE FROM BEYOND THE GRAVE.' Delete. Something indecipherable from accounts. Delete. Refresh. Delete.

"So. We have our 'learner' - who is a confederate, as you'll recall - in the chair. After he has learned a list of word pairs given him, the 'teacher' tests him by naming a word and asking the learner to recall its partner from a list of choices. And as for the teacher...the teacher is told to administer an electric shock every time the learner makes a mistake, increasing the level of shock each time. There are 30 switches on the shock generator marked from 15 volts (slight shock) to 450 (severe shock)."

He pauses, open-mouthed. I picture him as a deer about to be hit by a truck. I will him to run out of the room, but he finds his place in his scrawny notepad again.

"Well. I'm sure many of you can guess how this goes. The learner gives mainly wrong answers (on purpose) and for each of these the teacher must administer an electric shock."

We all know what happens. I doubt there's anyone in this room who hasn't read about fucking Milgram. It isn't a crochet convention. I unbutton my shirt at the neck. I'm hot these days; I'm always too hot. I think it might be The Weight.

"When the teacher refuses to administer a shock the experimenter – the actor – must give a series of orders or prompts. I had a slide with these on, but, er..."

He flips a page in his notebook, dropping his pen as he does. He stoops to pick it up and then stops, stands again and carries on.

"There are 4 prompts - or prods, if you will, haha - and if one was not obeyed then the experimenter must read out the next prod, and so on."

"Prod 1: Please continue. Prod 2: The experiment requires you to continue. Prod 3: It is absolutely essential that you continue...."

Prod 4: You have no other choice but to continue.

"Er, prod 4: You have no other choice but to continue."

I rearrange my bollocks conspicuously. He looks at me and then glances away quickly, as if he's embarrassed.

"Well," he says. "Would anyone like to hazard a guess - how many of the participants kept going, do you think? How many continued to 450 volts?"

Harry pipes up from the chair next to me. "65%."

Skinny-tie looks startled. "Uncanny. That's…. that's correct. 65%, two-thirds, of participants – i.e. teachers – continued to the highest level of 450 volts. All the participants continued to 300 volts. I'll just give that a moment to sink in."

Next to me, Harry is stifling a laugh. I wish someone would open a window. I feel like the rising mercury in a thermometer. My face is tipped red. It's The Weight, it gives me a flush. Like a coat I'm always wearing.

"Milgram…um, so Milgram did more than one experiment – he carried out 18 variations of his study. All he did was alter the situation."

The Weight started around the time we became successful. After that first meeting with The Prime Minister. The office with the black chairs. I remember him leaning across the table towards me, how my skin prickled in his presence. Thinking how much more like a waxwork he looked in real life. I remember his level voice: *it has come to our attention that the service your business provides may be able to assists us with a… statistical problem.*

"In summary, ladies and gentleman, what did Milgram prove? Well, I hope I have made it very clear. Ordinary people are likely to follow orders given by an authority figure, even to the extent of killing an innocent human being. Obedience to authority is ingrained in us all from the way we are brought up. People tend to obey orders from other people if they recognise their authority...."

That's what he had, the PM. An undeniable sense of authority. More than any dealer or gangster I ever met. His monotone. *I'm saying, we will be willing to draw a discreet veil over your operations from now on.* After that day, I did anything to avoid having to meet with him again. We had the nod from them. That was enough. *You must, of course, consider this endorsement unofficial. Do you understand me?*

The woman in the charcoal suit is asking a question about implicit authority versus imposed authority. I want a drink. I want to sit at the bar in a pub where nobody knows me and drink a bottle of shit house wine and eat bags of peanuts until the bar-staff kick me out. Just me and the flare of the jukebox. I want to switch my iPhone off.

"Would you say that it's important for the authority to feel earned?"

I never thought of myself as a businessman. When Harry suggested I should take the title CEO, I didn't even know what it stood for. When the website took off, I saw myself more as a glorified bouncer. Harry's the ideas man. He was the one who came up with the text, the branding. He was the one who looked up the Latin, invented the tagline. *Life plan facilitators.* Everything was discreet. Me, I'm about as discreet as Blackpool.

"That's an excellent question," skinny-tie says to the room. Then he repeats it back to her without really answering it.

We have business models and we have a five-year plan. We have Human Resources and support for writers, assassins, and psychologists. We have team building exercises involving replica bridges and matchstick towers. And we have corporate fucking training days.

In the car on the way back to the office, Harry puts Queen on the car stereo and flicks popcorn into his mouth. The inside of the car smells a bit like rotting fruit, old banana skins.

"I've never liked this song," I say and he turns the volume louder.

LORNA

I startle myself in the train toilet mirror. My eyes are held in two dark scoops, purplish. My face is taut - for the first time in my life, I have cheekbones. The sticker-writing across the glass says 'go on, give us a smile', so I frown at it. There's text above the toilet too: 'do not flush waste paper, dreams, goldfish, or your ex's sweater down here.' I don't know if I can bear a world where everything has to talk to you. Smoothie bottles. Shower gel, telling you what to do. Lather me. Drink me. Kill me now.

Nick Vincent is on the platform in a long tweed coat, a white shirt buttoned over his paunch. He takes his flat cap off as the train pulls in. I'm watching him look for me, scanning the crowd and I hold back for a moment. I notice he has a small, black satchel at his feet. A man bag. He's recently shaved and it doesn't entirely suit him. From a distance, there's something hard about his round face, but when he sees me, his jaw softens.

"Evening, my dear." Doncaster vowels. Two kisses, mock-continental. His aftershave is overpowering.

"Sorry I'm late."

He's already steering me down the platform. His hand touches the small of my back briefly and I flinch slightly in my light jacket.

"The support act are shit. We've still got time for a pint in The Feathers before 9."

One pint becomes two. I am parched. My skin feels thirsty and I want to plunge my head into the glass. I check my watch. Nick is talking about his son in London, his son who is older than me and more successful, working for a record label and living in Camden. He speaks about him with a detached clarity, without ever sounding fatherly. He leans towards me across the table at the end of each sentence. His eyes are very bright and very small, icy, as if they're being drowned by his face.

"Shouldn't we get going?"

He smiles. "If you insist." He holds out my jacket for me and I step into it.

Nick has a small, Moleskine notebook and a silver pen that he keeps clipped inside his coat. He writes nothing down through the whole gig, slipping back and forth from our row of seats to the bar instead. We've moved on to whiskey in squat, plastic cups. His breath is warm on my face when he leans across to speak to me over the bassline. The band are good, an act from Cleethorpes who sound like they're from 1950s America. Black flared skirts, a woman with a buttoned up cardigan, a bassist with an Elvis quiff. Their voices are deeper than them. Nick thinks he's whispering when he's shouting.

"When I started with the NME, there were nights when I never left the band's dressing room. Speed. Coke mostly, actually. I wrote the reviews in the toilets, standing up. Or I'd make them up the next day. You have to trust your instinct," he taps the side of his head. "Feel the music. In here."

I nod. I'm lost in private comparisons. Richard Hawley. The Black Keys, via Grimsby. I'm smiling, but not at Nick. He grins at me, his face distorted by the off-blue lights. He hasn't taken his coat off, even though the room is sweltering. I look at him sideways and try to imagine him younger, slighter, propping himself up backstage and talking to PJ Harvey. Nick's interviews are famous because they aren't really interviews, just conversations conducted at deliberate cross-purposes.

The band have four encores, each slower than the last.

"I don't hold with this shit," says Nick. "Poor man's Joss Stone. Too easy."

I smile. The last song is different, building to an insistent staccato rhythm, the drummer simmering the snare. The bassist turns his back to the audience and nods along in time, lost in the track's heartbeat. The singer grabs the mic stand with one hand and I wish I could be spontaneous on stage like that.

Nick takes my arm. "Dance with me."

I am drunker than I thought. We sway together, the swell of his stomach keeping us slightly apart. I tread on his toes twice, I stumble and he holds me up, laughing. A couple are looking at us, half-amused. I think of my dad teaching me to dance at a wedding when I was six, twirling me round in a dress that was printed with watermelons.

We miss the last train back to Nick's house, the tall terrace he inherited when his aunt died, the rooms with pink wallpaper he's hardly changed since. I've stayed there before after reviewing gigs, holed up on the hard camp bed and it always makes me think of my grandad's house in Oldham. There's a strange comfort in waking up there in the silence of the ex-pit town, birdless and bright. Tonight, we drink in a terrible bar called Sankeys, the kind of place I used to go to when I was seventeen, five bottles of tropical Reef for a fiver, a bored bouncer on the door, keeping his eyes fixed at arse-level. I'm animated, nostalgic, talking about nights out with Ginny, the time she got her hair curlers confiscated in a bar because they thought they were a weapon. Nick wears a bemused smile. There are seats but he chooses to stand up at a high table, leaning on it with a confidence I don't have. I've spoken too much. I'm embarrassed, running to a halt, but he tips his glass against mine.

"Drink up," He says. "I'll call us a taxi."

On the slow drive home, he tells me about the first gig of ours he ever saw. How funny I was, how strangely elegant in my awkwardness. He remembers some of our lyrics and I'm amazed, babbling about the writing process.

"I get ideas when I'm walking, when I'm late... I like to keep a line in my head and turn it over... you know, wear it down. A bit like chewing gum. I have to keep it going until there's no flavour left, until I've worked it properly. God, that makes our songs sound really bland, doesn't it?"

He has a deep laugh. "I know they aren't bland. You're a very talented lyricist. No word of a lie."

The taxi driver glances back. I meet his eyes in the thin mirror.

It is a weeknight. Everyone else is shut inside their houses, single bright lights on in the upstairs rooms. Only the garages are open. It feels decadent to be coming back from the noise of the gig and the late bar, closing my eyes and feeling like I'm always moving forwards. I ask if we can stop so I can get some cash. I'm tripping over my words slightly.

"Don't be ridiculous," says Nick. "I've got this."

I text my boyfriend to tell him I'm okay. *Gig was fucking brilliant. Nick was hilarious. Tell you tomorrow. Sleep tight, xxx* I stare at it too long to make sure I haven't drunk-spelled anything.

Nick unlocks the door for me and steers me firmly into his neat house. I am enthusiastic about everything. The framed black and white print of Bridlington, back in the day. The Nina Simone CD he puts on and the standing lamp that makes us golden, flattering my face. I feel Donny at night is the centre of a small universe. Nick has opened a bottle of coconut rum and the sickly smell reminds me of sun tan lotion as a kid. I wrap my cardigan tighter. We are close together on the leather sofa and I'm so tired I relax into it. Nick sits very close to one side of it, keeping his distance from me and I like that. His shirt is partly unbuttoned and the skin under the collar is slightly flushed. I look away, ask him questions about his vinyl collection. Almost everything in the house is signed. Even the glasses we're drinking from are scrawled with someone's signature, in permanent marker across the outside.

"Ruby Slippers," he says. "Remember them? I got Marg to sign these in '98."

"I never get anything signed. It's just a name. It could be anyone."

"You sound like a schoolgirl."

"No, girls at school want everything signed."

"Don't they just." He is looking at my chest, his stare burns. I am embarrassed for him. I pour myself more rum and we sit in separate silences for a moment, listening to Nina.

It is after 2-a.m. and I start to talk less, closing my eyes and letting Nick's voice lap over me. I nod and nod. I ask him the same questions but he doesn't notice, telling me the same story he told in Sankeys, the only story, the one about his painter ex wife and the riding accident, the battle with her family, what it was like being back in the house in Donny without her that first year. Three clear glass bottles in the bathroom, mementos from Suffolk he couldn't bring himself to throw out. Sea glass. Her winter coat hanging in the wardrobe like a curtain. I try to imagine Nick in love, try to imagine him haggard, driving, holding a child. I think of the last argument I had with my boyfriend. *I can't see you as a mother. I just can't.* People change shape to fill the glass of their lives. The glass of my life is full of coconut rum, translucent and sweet. I imagine the bottles Nick's dead wife collected high on a window shelf, letting the light through them in unbearably straight lines, morning light as a search beam. Light the colour of milk, of Malibu. I let the whiteness find me out, tuck me in, let it over my shoulders and over my face and hair.

When I wake up, I'm surrounded by the same paleness, but my body feels heavy. My face is pressed into the white of a pillow, the white of the sheets. I feel as if I'm being lifted, then I'm being pressed down, as if its snow around me instead of light. Nick is moaning, the sound is muffled, like voices through a wall. His grip is tight on my hips, there's something tangled around my leg. He slaps me, once twice, barely hard enough to feel and I hear my own voice, wordless, a low sound, indistinguishable from pleasure. I bury my face and let myself sink into the idea of a snowdrift, a bank of cold, the mound of winter I walked past one night behind the empty hospital, piled up against the wall, running my hand along it, surprised by how firm it was to the touch, how solid, how much less powdery than I imagined. I am under it now, burrowing and there's more warmth than I expected. It is me who is inside, going deeper and deeper, rooting through the brightness until I'm at the still heart of it and everything might as well be black. It feels like the same thing, staring at snow and staring at the sun. There is a groan escaping from my chest, one long note. When Nick forces my face down into the pillow, pulling my head and pushing it at the same time, his hand groping through my hair, I want him to hold me there, almost underwater. He shouts someone's name, not mine, and he pulls out, comes on the small of my back. I do not move. I stay on my knees, head down, open. I hear him get up and walk across the room.

"Put some clothes on," he says. He shuts the bedroom door behind him.

The night I found the hospital snowdrift, I remember I scrambled to climb on top of it and sat for a while as if it was a hill fort, watching the steam rise from the laundry building, thinking of whoever was inside, working quietly through the small hours. It was very silent. Nobody was arriving in an ambulance. Nobody was smoking outside the lit reception. I stayed until I was damp, chilled, imagining how easy it would be to never get up again. I walked home with a pebble of ice in my hand. It kept for a long time before it thawed and trickled down my jeans.

JAMIE

"Look at me, Dad!"

Light comes through the domed windows and turns this place into a greenhouse. Relentless light. I don't remember having the chance to learn, but I must have done. Swimming lessons after school, the tiled baths on Foljambe Road echoing with shrieks and the sound of some kid slapping the water, the sting of his skin. Belly-flop. That's what we used to call it. I remember the changing rooms, the art of trying to take your trunks off under your towel, but not the water. Maybe I just stood in the shallow end and never spoke.

"Look, Dad, I can butterfly!"

Rowan is churning through the water, making huge furrows on either side of him. He turns his face in a gasp and his green goggles make him look like a bluebottle. He almost takes out a kid in armbands.

'Careful, Ro," I mutter from the side, but his ears are full of the rush of water. I'm up to my waist and that's far enough.

A couple of teenagers are treading water in the deep end. She's got peroxide blonde hair, almost silver, and whenever she paddles towards him they sneak a kiss. Rowan careers past them, soaking her. A bald man in tight Speedos is slinking up and down the fast lane, separated from the rest of us by a line of orange beads, a bracelet of them. The lifeguard sits in his eyrie and looks down. Mick Price. Year below me at school.

"Dad, Dad!" Rowan gulps. "I'm doing it!"

I give him the thumbs up as he ploughs back towards me, swallowing water.

"I'm a butterfly!"

"More like a moth-man," I yell and I puff my cheeks out and show him my tongue. He steers himself to a halt near me and hits the water in front of him with his hands, sending a small wave up over my chicken-pale chest.

Mick Price sounds his shrill whistle. "No splashing!"

No heavy petting. No bombing. No food. No drinks. No running on the poolside.

"Watch me dive!" says Rowan, flickering under the surface.

Even the chubbiest boy in the class could swim. Simon, with red weals of acne across his shoulders and back, a small universe of spots and scars. He stood unashamed in the showers, letting the steam rise from him. I don't remember being in the showers, just watching from somewhere by the lockers. I remember the metal steps of the poolside, the slow lowering, but I don't remember the chill of the pool.

It's always like that. The car journey, but not the destination. The gin, but not the hotel room. The way I can bring back everything with my eyes shut when we're apart, everything except Julia's face.

Zoe isn't here, so I don't know why I'm imagining her sitting up in the red plastic seats and watching us, wondering how she married a man who can't swim. Fiddling absently with her false thumbnail, picking it off. I think I'd look better from above. I imagine it a lot - when I'm having sex, mostly, or when I'm driving. As if I'm staring down on myself. As if I'm standing on the top diving board, the widest one of the three, the one that hardly bends. I'm right on the edge, and there's a kid behind me threatening to push me if I don't jump, but I'm mesmerised by the small sight of myself, down there.

That never happened, not the thing with the kid and the diving board.

Rowan bobs up metres off like a seal and disappears again. He swims underwater and grabs me by the leg, then ripples away. When he comes up, his hair is otter-smooth against his head.

I crouch down so that the water touches my shoulders and I inch away from the side. If I've swum once, my body must remember. Like riding a bicycle, or being in a car. Like walking. Like sleep. There's nothing to be afraid of. I've made it through this year alive. The baths are illuminated and my face is warm. I realise I've been holding my breath and I let some of it out through my nose. I start to push off.

For a second, I'm afloat. I'm really doing it, I'm moving with my feet off the ground. That's when the fire alarm sounds and the air become shrill. Mick springs down from his perch, legs and arms elastic.

"Everyone out!" he bawls. "Evacuate!"

An older lady is crossing herself as a lad helps to lift her up the steps. Children are screaming and jostling and a mother swoops down to lift one of them by the arm, gripping too tight. I've got hold of Rowan's hand and we half-wade, half-scramble. I grab a towel from the poolside - I don't know who it belongs to - and wrap it round him.

Out in the car park, we're filed into shivering lines. Drivers on the main road slow down to gawp at us. The alarm from the building is still singing and receptionists in red polo neck t-shirts and tailored trousers are bunched together, one of them still holding a sandwich. It isn't a cold day, but the children are shuddering. I pull the towel over Rowan's shoulders, a blue, soft quilt.

"That's mine," says a woman with a collapsed perm. "That's my best beach towel." But she makes no attempt to take it back.

My cock is shrinking in my baggy swimming trunks and my arms are stippled with goosebumps. A year ago, I'd have found this humiliating. A year ago, I found the sight of my own profile in a shop window unbearable. The breath filling my chest when I lay flat on my back in the mornings, like a grotesque balloon. Now, I just want to laugh. Mick is parading round the car park waving his arms like an orchestra conductor. Occasionally, a driver passes and beeps at us, or someone rolls down their window to shout and I give them the thumbs up.

I'm thinking of the first Christmas after I met Julia. That late December, when I'd decided I didn't want to die. I bought lavish presents for everyone that year. A pedal-powered car for Rowan. A gold chain for Zoe and some Gucci perfume in a squat, metallic bottle. On Christmas Day, I walked on my own to The Butchers Arms and sank three neat gins with ice. Outside on the concrete square that passed for a beer garden, two paunchy men in their late forties were sunbathing topless on the ground under the winter sun, identical pints of Fosters balanced on the ground next to them. I brought the tumbler to my lips and breathed in the smell of juniper and thought about Julia, the taste of her, that night in the beige and cream hotel. The night that was meant to be my last.

Mick is striding up and down the lines like a drill sergeant. He seems to slow down as he passes me and Rowan and I wonder if he remembers. I think about stopping him, saying the name of our school and form. A woman behind me in the line is wailing now, asking when we'll be allowed back in.

That's when I see her out of the corner of my eye. As if thinking about her has summoned her. She's in a grey wool coat, coming out of the park and cutting through towards town. She has a bag slung from her shoulders and another in her hand, plastic. She turns her head.

"Julia," I didn't mean to say it out loud.

She stops and stares, then she hitches her rucksack up on her shoulder and walks on, under the shelter of the trees. The silvery trunks seem to move slightly as I look at them. Leafless. Like tuning forks. In that coat, she's a pale image of herself, ghosting between them.

I know there'll be a text message later. I know she couldn't come over. But for a moment, I'm gripped by that old sensation, the one I haven't felt since we met. I want to turn to see her again, make sure she's still there. I need to know she exists. It's as if there's tepid water in my stomach and it rises to fill my empty lungs and throat, spreads through my chest. That's what it used to be like - not like drowning, but someone's idea of drowning. Like a boy on the side at the deep end who doesn't know whether or not he can swim, the tiled walls sweating, the calls of the others getting further and further away until he kids himself he must be under the surface after all. Imagining the choke and clutch of the water as it coaxes him down.

The high-pitched siren cuts out and the receptionists start clapping. Julia is not in the woods, not passing the skeletal bandstand.

"Ok," says Mick. "Everybody back in."

He walks a step behind us, shooing everyone in. Then he pauses.

"Do I know you?"

I reach down for Rowan's arm and I shake my head.

LORNA

The year Ginny vanished. September had no clouds. We'd not finished carving our names into the oak tree, though we'd stripped the bark where we meant to do it, a smooth, bald patch, slightly green, big enough to place your hand in. If you look, even now, you'll see it just has her initials. G.L. Very fine with her dad's penknife. She held it under my chin once, the way you'd hold a buttercup there to see if someone liked butter.

We were playing a game with her little brother Paul. His favourite. I had to close my eyes and count to twenty and they would sprint down the hill together and hide in the pub grounds, in the thatch of weeds that used to be a bowling green, or the mouth of the shattered cricket pavilion.

I took my hands away from my face. Everything was still. Like the middle of the night, but the sky was that weak blue daytime colour and the sun touched my shoulders. Often, they went into the pub building and hid in the downstairs function room with its frayed purple carpets and stacks of chairs with missing seats. They'd giggle when I came in, and burst out through the pile.

I only got nervous when Ginny led him down the lane to hide behind the farm hedges or crouch in the ditch. Mum said I shouldn't take that track. It led over the dip, through mining country, places where the winding wheels used to be. There were deep trenches and signs that said *deep water, keep out.* Once, Ginny saw a man there, asleep on his way back from the pub. She said he breathed like a horse.

I found Paul at the foot of the oak tree, gripping his hands around his knees. He was facing downhill, towards the thin line of hawthorn that marked the end of the pub grounds and the start of wilder fields, places where you saw foxes and rabbits at dusk. There was a breeze then, and all his blonde hair stood on end. He wouldn't say anything to me, but he never spoke much anyway. He was a kid, a real kid, not like me and Ginny with our tape collections and borrowed lipstick. I looked up into the branches, expecting her to leap down.

I always thought the oak tree must have a secret door in it, an outline that appeared in the right light, letting you down through a trap of roots. I thought it would be the perfect hiding place.

I looked at the haze over the fields and tried to imagine it as a curtain. I couldn't. The ground was solid. But there must be hidden doorways in our town. There must be holes in the sky for the stars to get through. There are places you go if you don't want to be found.

*

When I was eighteen, like everyone on our street, I got a tattoo. It was a bad design, a rose with an arrow through it. My initials underneath. I didn't tell mum. I went out early one Saturday and shrank into my jacket on the bus. It was raining and the market square was dense with umbrellas. We never had a market anymore, but the stalls were still there, candy-striped. September. That sense of things starting, like you've not disappointed yourself yet. I was in a punk covers band at college and we had a gig that week, a wedding. I wanted that tattoo to be healed by then so I could show it off.

The tattooist was Gary Brooks. He was in my year at school but not my form. He had a lank ponytail scraped back off his head and a blue stud in one ear. He held his arms away from his body slightly, as if he wanted to look bigger. As I signed the forms, he squinted at me.

"Don't I recognise you?"

I shook my head. The parlour was noisy, a droning, knitting kind of sound.

"Which school did you go to?"

"Parklands Academy."

I glanced at my feet. I always flushed when I lied.

In the back room, there was a man in his forties lying on his back with his t-shirt off. I watched his stomach rise and fall as the tattooist leaned over him, then sat back and wiped the blood away.

The walls were papered with black and white designs, intricate line drawings. A coiled serpent with a flickering tongue, almost as long as its body. A wolf, square on top of a jagged mound of rocks - the raised detail of its fur. Two bears, locked together in a fight. Next to them was a missing persons poster, a lad with a shaved head and an open, cheerful face.

The autumn when Ginny vanished, there were posters all around the centre for weeks, at bus stops and post offices, in the windows of pubs. Her mother went on TV and broke down in tears. There was an article in the paper with Ginny's school photograph: she beamed from the front page with her small teeth. Then winter came and there was someone else. A boy from Middlewood called Steven. Or Stewart. Another smiling face. Nobody talked about Ginny any more. I saw her mum once in the corner shop in the village, loaded down with carrier bags. She pushed straight past me as she left and slammed the door, the bell jangling.

Gary Brooks didn't say anything as he sat me down on the cling-film-wrapped chair and bent over the sink, putting on his gloves. I remembered him leaning back into the brickwork of the science block, pulling a packet of fags from his pocket, offering one to Ginny as she giggled and flipped her hair over her shoulder. He was taller than the other boys in our year, like Ginny was taller than the other girls. Once, in chemistry, he reached over from the seat behind and unhooked my bra and I felt sweat trickle down my breasts. I folded my arms tight and tried to stop the fabric riding up over my nipples. Another time, Gary and his friend Simon picked me up and carried me behind the sports hall, planting me in a bin. All the pencils and books in my school bag tipped out and I scrabbled around for them. A wasp flew out of the bin and bothered my shoulder. I remembered Ginny's shriek - *a tampon! She's got a tampon in her bag!*

Gary Brooks adjusted the seat.

"Lie on your front," he said. "And take your t-shirt off."

I pulled my top up, lifting the back over my head first so my chest was covered until last, the way I used to before PE. Getting changed next to Ginny at school, I always tried not to look at her long back and thin neck. I was a child. My shoulders were square. My hair was cut shorter than I wanted it. I wore stretched crop tops and Ginny wore lace-trimmed bras, beaded in the middle with bows or tiny pearls.

I lay face down on the chair and turned my face to one side. The round man across the room was staring at me so I shifted my head the other way. I could hear Gary opening a packet, then testing the needle, a dull whine.

"Ready?"

It wasn't pain I felt, more insistence. Something pushing at me, trying to get in. I imagined the shape of a flower, imagined the petals, one by one. Every now and then, Gary would pause and I could hear him breathing.

"You work at Rush, don't you?"

I was surprised. I'd never clocked him there, jostling with the others at the bar. I would have noticed him, his height and his slimness, that look he always wore, as if he was about to leave. But my town is like that. You can blend in if you want to. The clubs are a good place to be lost.

"It's just a summer thing. I'm going to Uni soon. Music." I paused. "You might have seen my band. We played the Labour Club. Last week, actually."

As soon as I said it, I wished I hadn't. He went back to my shoulder, carving gently, brushing at the skin when it bled. I became conscious of my hair, the stale, smoky smell from last night's shift.

"Right then, pal, you're done." It was the other tattooist.

The fat man heaved to a sitting position and hosted himself up. He admired himself in the mirror, his chest red around the ink: a tiger with one reaching paw, stretched out towards his heart, its mouth curled into a snarl. Then the tattoo parlour was quiet apart from the sound of Gary's needle. He was pausing more often, taking his time. I felt like I was being watched. But there was nobody except Gary.

When he stopped, I went to sit up, but he put his hand against the small of my back. He crouched down next to me so that he was level with my ear. My head was facing the other way and I wanted to turn round to look at him but I didn't dare. I thought he was going to kiss me. I could smell cigarettes on his breath, the stale, fruity smell of last night's cider.

"I've seen her," he said. "She's here."

I didn't speak. I didn't move. I could hear the other tattooist out in the front room, rummaging behind the desk and whistling.

"Don't say you don't know who I mean, Lorna."

The way he said my name, he made it sound like an afterthought. The way Ginny always used to say it.

"She's squatting in a house off the ring road. She's dyed her hair. But you'll know her."

I thought about the day the police came round and mum made them cups of tea. *Did Ginny say anything unusual to you that day, Lorna? Do you remember what she was wearing?* The silence in the corridors when I came back to school. The lowered voices. *Maybe she did. Maybe Speccy did her in.*

"Well," Gary said loudly, standing up. "Let's get some cling-film on that rose for you. Have a look in the mirror, see what you think."

I stood carefully in front of the glass and peered over at my shoulder. It was branded, crimson and small.

I turned to face Gary. I started to say something. My mouth went dry.

He turned to the side and started peeling off his gloves, the fingers smudged with red ink.

"Make sure you keep it clean. Wash it three times a day. Cream afterwards. We sell stuff out front."

*

The club was the busiest it had been all summer. The air was stifling outside and people brought the heat in on their bodies and breath. The bouncers were short-tempered and said nothing when I took them their cans of Red Bull. There was a fight by nine o' clock and someone lost his teeth.

At eleven, I was serving a pair of men at the bar - they leaned like brothers, matching jawlines and piss-hole eyes. I stooped to fetch their drinks, and when I turned back, one had glassed the other over the head. The first man stood over him, quietly, as if he couldn't work out how it had happened. The ambulance came and they carried him away without a fuss. That was how it was on Fridays.

After that, Karen sent me to the cellar to top up the stock. I stood next to the crates, relishing the coolness of it, that fermented smell, the bassline shaking the ceiling. My shoulder was smarting, the rose starting to prickle and itch. I stayed there for as long as I could get away with, thinking about the end of summer and packing my bags and never working here again, never hearing these songs, never lying in bed at home with my ears ringing and my blood loud. *You can come back whenever you like*, the manager had said. *People usually do in the end.*

I heaved a crate of cherry VK and staggered up the stairs with it. When I pushed my way through the door, the music slapped me. The DJ was playing 'Ride On Time' and there were bodies everywhere, women taking their stilettos off and jumping in bare feet the way they never jumped for the band, never jumped at gigs.

When I saw her, I dropped the crate. She was at the downstairs bar, the one that never had a queue, even on nights like this, and she was hunched over it, her face curtained by hair. I recognised her by her shoulders and her long neck. I shoved the crate to one side and pushed through the dancers. My heart was skittering in my chest. I thought about Gary and wondered what he'd said, wondered if he'd lied to me, if they were living together. Ginny was always good at acting. When she tripped me in the basement of the pub, or pushed me over and pulled my hair, she pretended to cry afterwards.

I was close to her now and I hesitated. The DJ had switched to a slow song and the club seemed to murmur with it. It had been six years. The town had forgotten her face. She'd been gone just long enough to slip back in, nudge between the bodies at the bar and take her place.

I stood behind her left shoulder. The glow from the optics made her blue. She must have sensed me but she didn't stir. Across town, people would be piling into taxis, driving up the four dark hills out to the villages, the lights getting smaller and smaller behind them. By next month, I'd be gone. There are towns like mine everywhere. Places nobody says they come from. Places that used to be built on coal or steel or cotton, where you can live on the suburbs and never say a word. But she'd chosen here.

I put my hand on her shoulder.

"Ginny?" I said

The face that turned to mine was like no-one I'd ever seen.

MAUREEN

Not your voice but the voice of an Irish poet I heard on the wireless once. Like he had treacle in his throat. Not the smell of warm milk but the milky light on the garden, most mornings for at least half an hour. Not the taste of bread but the feeling of cutting it. Like that - the way the knife almost snags on the crust then sinks into the dough.

Not driving to cities but driving into them, the ragged outskirts and uptight suburbs. Not the hour before sleep or the first hour after. None of it. Not even sleep itself. Not beaches but islands, scoured places without trees. Not hot coffee but cold tea. Tea with whisky. Not the music but the moment after the song, the stiller silence. I suppose that's a cliché. I suppose that's what everyone would say. Tom Waits, when he stops singing.

Not being drunk but the first few sips of red wine, the warmth before the numbness. Not the stars but the changeable moon. And not the sky but the weather passing across it. Fine rain, beading my eyebrows. Not chess, I won't even miss chess, but the shape of the rooks. The pawns I could fold into my hand, completely. Not talking to my brother but listening to him laugh on the phone. Not whisky but the stink of it in the glass, next day - lifting the glass to douse it under the tap, the kitchen full of peat. Not shoes but socks. Not scarves but hats, head-hugging hats and oversized, inappropriate ones. Not the news but the faces of the newsreaders. Never the news. And not reading books but holding them, weighing them on my palm. Smelling them sometimes.

Not your letters but opening them. Not the memory of you but the thought of you in your small house by the crossroads. Not the road north but the motorway signpost that says THE NORTH. Not the bridge but the way the water used to pulse under it in sunlight and shadow. Not the hope in your eyes but the kindness. Not your accent but the pitch of your voice. Not boiled sweets but toffees, thick and claggy, the way they silence people in cars. Not your answers but the way you'd ask a question and then turn back to your food. Not the baby and not the bathwater. Rose water, its subtlety. Not oranges but satsumas. Not this, definitely not this.

BRIAN

I'm carrying it to my chest, like a child. The lass pushing her mountain bike must wonder what I've got under my jacket. I didn't bring a bag and the urn was too thick for my pocket. I nod to her and keep walking up the asphalt track. The reservoir seems very flat from here, beaten silver.

"Morning," I say under my breath, though I'm not really speaking to her or anyone. "Beautiful day."

It is, mind. So cold the whole landscape seems preserved. Saddleworth under a salt layer of frost. My feet hardly make an impression on the hard ground. I'm walking up towards Wimberry Stones. Indian's Head we called it, when I was a kid. I feel funny saying that now. When you look at the rocks in profile, you can imagine it - a stately, craggy kind of face with a jutting nose, the face of a village elder. Indian Chief, I guess that's what they were thinking of. In 1949, a Dakota plane crashed here on the way to Manchester in bad fog. Hardly any survivors. I grew up with stories like that the way I grew up on tales about Alderman and Alphin, two giants hurling stones at each other across the valley, each trying to knock the other one out. I used to like thinking of the landscape like that. One big chessboard for the Gods and us just lurking in it or passing through. It helps, seeing things that way. It has lately.

A hare goes skittering across the moor, back into safe undergrowth. A hare or a rabbit. The clouds plume over its absence, conjuror's smoke. Once as a nipper I was here with Dad and we found this moving patch of ground. I touched it with my boot and the whole surface wobbled. Alien. I prodded it again, scared I'd break through the surface, but it just rippled. Later, we found out it was methane, trapped under the ground. I came back to look for it, but I could never quite place the spot again.

Moors are like that. Shifting. Tricksy. If you leave something up here, the ground might swallow it. When I was a kid, the police came to our door. The Moors murders. Myra Hindley and the other one, I don't recall his name now. They'd found bodies up past the village, graves in the moor, somewhere near Hollin Brown Knoll. They knocked on doors, the coppers. It was when they were still looking for graves, after they'd been done. They reckon there's a body somewhere that they never found. Keith somebody. I remember his photograph, black and white.

Driving back towards Saddleworth for the first time after I'd married, moved to Sheffield, I saw the moors as if I'd never looked at them properly before. Max was in the back seat, strapped in. Well, half strapped in - they weren't as strict in those days. It was raining like buggery, the kind of weather that seems to have hands, rain and wind gripping the car and trying to nudge it over. You couldn't tell the land from the mist. I felt that dip in my stomach as the car dropped down over the hill and, when I looked over towards Greenfield, I realised I'd never clocked it before, how dark the moors were. How they could look almost... I won't say evil, but brooding. In the pub car park, I pulled a woollen hat on and wrapped Max up warm and tucked him into his carrier and hitched him onto my back. I had to lean into the weather all the way up the track and from time to time I stopped to check on him, make sure he was warm enough. The carrier was a bit flimsy and we'd dropped him out of it once before. It makes you feel like a terrible parent saying that now. Anyhow, he slept nearly all the way. I didn't see another soul for hours, not until I got back down to the village. After that, I never really went back. Sundays, we'd walk up Kinder from Hayfield, or go to Hollins Cross and Mam Tor from Castleton, stop at the caverns afterwards, have a cuppa in the cafe. I don't know where Max got it from, his love of this place, or why he started coming back as a teenager. Maybe it's in the blood.

Last year, they found the body of a bloke up here on the track, right where the ground its boggiest. Right where I am now. He was lying with his head pointing towards the top of Wimberry and his legs together and his arms stiff by his sides. Cold. They reckon he had nothing in his pockets but some train tickets from Manchester to Euston, a hundred quid or so and an empty bottle of medicine printed in English and Urdu. He was wearing blue cords and a light jacket, a pair of black Bally loafers on his feet. They cost a bob or two. He'd been into the Clarence, asked the way to the rocks. Nobody could trace him, still haven't. But when they tested the bottle later, they found traces of strychnine in it. It's not a peaceful death.

The letter that Max left - the letter they sent me, I don't think he wrote it - told me about the method he'd chosen. 'Service' they called it, actually. It wasn't a long letter, but he never had much to say so they got that right. I couldn't read it for a month. Kept it folded up in the drawer of the bedside cabinet. I looked at the words but I didn't take them in. When I finally picked it up, that was the only part I cared about - how he went. Whether it was calm. Whether it was quick.

The landlord of the Clarence said the man who set off walking to Indian's Head that day had a northern accent but he didn't sound like he was from round here. He didn't want a drink, left quickly. It was almost dark already by the time he started out and the mist was tucking in the hillside. *It rained all day the day before and it rained all day the day after.* The man in the mac asked him to repeat the directions and then he was gone.

When I was small, my dad used to take me to the museum. I think it was near Diggle, or maybe near Dobcross. It might have been somewhere bigger than either of those places and we went there on the bus. What I do remember is that there was a tank in the corner of the stuffy, airless room with snakes in it. I could never work out why they were there - there were no other animals or reptiles, just plaques about local history, sepia pictures of carthorses and mill workers. I'd run straight for the tank, never wanted to look at anything else. One day, the snakes weren't there and there were just these two white husks, long and papery, coiled near the glass. I think I cried. But they were only hiding, tightly wound somewhere far back in the sawdust. They'd slunk back and left their old skins behind, like clues. I always wish I'd taken Max there, found out where the museum was before it closed down.

When Max was little, he used to play hide and seek on his own out back in our garden. We didn't have many trees, nothing much good for hiding behind and he always seemed upset by that. As if the terraces had no mysteries. I sometimes thought about what it would have been like to bring him up here, with the silence and the broken face of the outcrop and the pewter sky. When he left home and we heard from him less and less, I used to think of it like that - a game of hide and seek. A countdown until he'd come out again.

There was nothing in the note that explained anything. Not really.

I see it out of the corner of my eye first. A long, thick shape by the bracken. Almost like an alligator. I nearly drop the urn, catch up, grip it close again. The half-sunken feet. One knee raised slightly. The seal-slick shape of the head.

"Hey!"

I don't know who I'm shouting to. I'm alone, plunging off the track. I go down into the mud, up to my calves. The ground drags at me.

"Hey. Hey...." The sound comes out of me like a laugh.

He faces the sky, shrunken with cold. The crows wheeling in the distance haven't touched him. I stumble forwards, right boot almost sucked off by the muck. I want to put my hands on him, grip him by the torso and shake him, put my hands under his armpits and haul him up. I want to look him in his marble eyes. I realise I am muttering under my breath.

Up close, he is a scarecrow. Smaller than he looked. I am clinging on to the urn, one hand under my jacket and the other flailing forwards. I think about the bodies preserved in peat for centuries, how the ground shrivels and holds them. I imagine a plane crashing into the ground and tunnelling, down under the surface. The prone bodies. The single boy who crawled from the fuselage, crawled over men who lay like this: skyward, cooling skin.

I am on my knees now and it's all I can do to hold the urn, stop things spilling out, keep Max close to me. I reach forwards with my free arm and I touch the dead man's skin. Gnarled bark. A dampness where the water seeped in. Rivulets across the surface of the wood. I kneel next to what's left of the tree and I howl.

I don't know how long I'm there. When the rain starts, I pick myself up and walk back to the path with sodden boots and dark jeans. I look back at the tree trunk, laugh.

I should be on top of the edge, high on Indian's Head, but I'm down below it, overshadowed by it, staring up. It reminds me of an old man's skin. Circular holes, like sunken eye sockets, or hollows where a collarbone might be. *Stop it.* I hit myself in the face. *Stop seeing things.* The missing man, the fella they started calling Neil Dovestone had a craggy face, distinctive nose. Something ancient about him. I wonder how old people think I am when they look at me. I feel ancient. Old enough to have outlived a son.

I don't need to climb any further. I'm out of puff. Standing with my back to the outcrop, I let myself look down the path, let my gaze settle on the bunched houses of Greenfield. A few houses. A pub. That's all. I take my hand from the top of the urn and say his name, just once, and I let what's left of my boy go.

LORNA

Because I'm with Ginny, the fall doesn't look that bad. Or that far. The railway tracks stretch away into the distance past the scrap yard and the place where all the buses go when they're worn out and I follow the parallel lines with my eyes until I can't imagine there's any part of the world they don't circle.

Train tracks, that's what they call the metal on my teeth. The earth is wearing braces. High on the bridge, I wiggle further out so that my hips are leaning against the bricks and I tilt forwards, letting my hair fall over my face and the blood rush to my head. Then I tip back, hitch myself up until I'm sitting on the edge, turn round to face the tracks again with my feet dangling down. Ginny hoists herself beside me. It's blazing hot and she smells of strawberry laces and banana shampoo, the stuff her mum buys from The Body Shop.

"I still dare you," she says. "You're chicken."

She's wearing cola lip balm and her mouth is pale red and shiny. She's got a bit on her chin, a slick of colour.

I look down at the drop. The metal glints. "I'll do it if you do it."

"Cheat," says Ginny. "Cheeeeeaaaat."

Then she pinches me on the arm, not hard, but enough to make my skin bloom.

"Cheat, cheat, cheat." I think of the sound the trains make when they go past the back of our house. Like that. Or like the playground at our old school. Chanting. Like the trains know a secret.

Ginny leans over, rests her head on my shoulder. Her blonde hair is warm and sickly. She nuzzles me with her face, pretending to wipe her nose on me.

"Kidding," she says. "If you jumped, I'd come too. I'd jump right after you did."

"Liar."

She laughs, hooks one of her legs over the side of the wall so she's straddling it, turned towards me. She gets a tin out of the pocket of her black dungarees and holds it open.

"Cig?"

They're very slim and long, fronds of tobacco poking out of the ends.

"I'm ok."

"Go on," she takes one and prods me with it. "I rolled them myself."

Ginny's boyfriend taught her how to roll because he's four years older and has a scooter and gets the house to himself at weekends. She disappears with him after school, somewhere on the walk between the garage and Fryars chip shop. Sometimes, I'm dawdling and pretending not to watch them holding hands and when I turn they've gone. Last night, they showed up at my house with a six-pack of Strongbow. Ginny rang the bell while he waited at the end of the garden path, like he was too shy to come to the door. We saved two cans and had them this morning on the walk over to the bridge. We threw the empties at each other and ducked. Summer snowball fight.

Ginny throws her head back like a film star and blows smoke

towards the sun. I'm still struggling to light mine.

"It's too hot to smoke," she says.

We sit in silence and I kick my legs, thinking about how - close up - the end of Ginny's cig looks as big as the sun. I don't tell Ginny some of the things I keep in my head in case she makes fun of me, which is stupid, because she never thinks anything is strange. Sometimes I want to lift the lid on my brain like a cigarette tin. Ginny's is red and white and it says 'FUCK THE RICH, FUCK THE POOR' across the front.

"Okay," murmurs Ginny. "Would you rather..."

"Not now." I blow my smoke in her face.

When Ginny talks, she stretches one of her arms out as if she's conducting an invisible orchestra. There's a low hedgerow with blackberries in it by the left of the tracks and just now her arm and the hedge are the same angle. I like it when I notice things. Stuff like that. It's how it feels when I'm writing a song. One thing finding another and underlining it.

"Would you rather jump off this bridge or be pushed into a six foot pile of shit?"

I narrow my eyes. "Bridge."

"Would you rather... kiss Damon Smith or shag his dad?"

"You're disgusting."

"Would you rather..."

"It's my turn," I flick ash from my rollie and watch it drift towards the tracks until I can't see it any more. The metal down there must be red hot. "Would you rather burn to death or freeze?"

"Easy," Ginny gets her lighter out again. "Freezing's like going to sleep."

I hop down from the wall and make her follow me. On the other side of the bridge, there's a bank where you can see back across the fields. My dad reckons it's the dividing line between two counties. Ginny lingers for a moment, stubs her fag out against the brick. Her shadow overtakes me before she catches up.

"Would you rather shoot me or shoot yourself?" she says in my ear. Then she laughs.

On the bank, we lie on our backs and the long, pale grass scratches at me, my neck and legs. Ginny isn't bored yet. Ginny never gets bored.

"Would you rather... have tongues for fingers or a big finger for a tongue?"

I close my eyes and I can still see the sun. I stick my tongue out and try to imagine it could curl around straws, clutch at things. Then I stroke my own nose and think about having wet fingertips.

"That's sick," I say. "You're sick. Imagine tasting everything you touched."

"Imagine tasting Damon's P.E. kit."

I make a gagging noise.

"If you had tiny tongues for fingers, you might not need to eat anything. You'd just stroke a plate of chips and that would be enough." Ginny has turned on her side towards me and she's propping herself up with her elbow.

"I think I'd have a finger for a tongue," I say. "Just to see what kissing was like."

Ginny sniggers. "How would you know the difference?"

"I've kissed loads of people."

"Bullshit."

That's when Ginny leans over and presses her sweet-sticky lips against mine. It only lasts for a moment. Fruit and smoke. Her tongue glancing over my teeth, touching the roof of my mouth. Her lips catch my braces and she doesn't flinch.

"Bare your teeth," she whispers. "Show me your teeth."

I grimace, clamp my teeth together. Then she puts her hands on the back of my neck and leans forward and traces the top line of my braces with her tongue, up-and-down movements, like handwriting. She does the same with the bottom row.

"Open your mouth" she says, and her tongue slips inside again, strokes mine gently. That's what it feels like - stroking.

I reach up and hold her head. Her hair's soft but dry. She reminds me of my teddy bear, Pepper, the one I pretend I don't have and I'm embarrassed for thinking that. As if she knows, she pulls away.

"You kiss better than James," she laughs.

A plane passes overhead and divides the sky in two. No trains go past. I wonder if there ever are any. If I was up on the bridge again, I think I'd jump this time, just to see what happened. I don't reckon it would hurt. I feel as if my bones are made of bricks and the ground won't smash me.

All day, I've been carrying a song. I ask Ginny if she wants to hear it and she says of course she does. I pull the paper out of my pocket and I start to say the words out loud, very slowly at first:

At the back of my mind
There's a thought of you.
It tastes of lemon rind,
Smells of barbecues.

I pause. Ginny is sitting up, hugging her knees. She's between me and the sun. "Go on," she says.

But you don't burn.
No, you don't burn.

I take a deep breath and feel the whole hot afternoon in my lungs. I feel like I did when I was writing it, in the kitchen after school with the clock louder than ever in the background and the rest of the house still. I don't know who 'you' is. I didn't think of anyone when I wrote it. Maybe it would be better if I made someone up.

In the mirror at night
You look back at me
And you're hairless and light
Like a winter tree

But you don't turn.
No, you don't turn.

When I hold my breath
I can hold your name
Burn its match to death
Like my tongue's a flame

But you don't burn.
Not really, you don't burn.

I realise I'm singing it instead of speaking, quiet singing. I don't have a good voice, but it sounds better this way.

I step into you
You're my favourite coat
I'll roll up the truth
Push it down my throat

And I'll never turn,
No, I'll never turn away.

Ginny doesn't face me for a minute. She puts her hands on top of her knees like she's balancing the song on them. Then she leans her head. "Give it here, will you?"

She's hunched over the paper, murmuring things aloud.

"In the third... verse, is it? Third verse. You used 'burn' again. Might be better with something else."

She takes another cig from the tin and lights it, passes it over to me.

"'Run its match to death'," she says. Then she smiles. "Don't listen to me. It's already beautiful."

"It's shit."

"Never let anyone tell you that. Promise me something, Lorna?" She's serious now, her face has dropped. I meet her stare. "Don't listen to anyone who tells you you're shit. Least of all you."

I love the smell of smoke on my skin. Afterwards. When I'm at home.

"You're a great writer."

We lie on the bank for hours, tanning ourselves. We fall asleep back to back and when we wake up we've got sunburn and the evening's cool in the grass and on our shins.

We walk home very slowly. There's a bank behind my house where we used to go tobogganing when we were kids, on snow days at school. Sacks and bin liners, things my mum found in the shed. It isn't a steep hill, but it's long. Ginny lies down first and I give her a shove and she goes rolling away from me, faster and faster, hair spinning. I go next. It's better than a rollercoaster. It lasts longer. At the bottom, we're covered in grass and my denim shorts are stained bright green. We get up and sprint to the top and we do it again. I think about egg rolling at school every Easter - painting the shells and bowling them. Some would break and some wouldn't.

At the gate, I tell her I'll see her tomorrow as she turns to wave. When she's gone, I realise she still has the song in her pocket.

Thanks and Acknowledgements

Thanks to the following publications where versions of some of these stories first appeared: *Now Then, New Walk magazine.*

Thank you to Alan Buckley, Chris Neilan, Mark Pajak and Ian Cartland for reading early versions of these stories and to Rachel Genn for encouraging me to believe in them. Thanks most of all to Joe Hakim for feedback and for giving me the confidence to pursue the idea behind this collection in the first place.